For my parents

CROSSING

Andrew Xia Fukuda

PUBLISHED BY

amazon encore

The characters and events portrayed in this book are fictitious. Any similarity to real persons, living or dead, is coincidental and not intended by the author.

Author Photo by Justin Ong www.jongphoto.com

Published by AmazonEncore
P.O. Box 400818
Las Vegas, NV 89140

ISBN-13: 9781935597032
ISBN-10: 1935597035

ACKNOWLEDGMENTS

I am indebted to many for their help and encouragement over the years. Specifically, I wish to thank:

My indefatigable editor, Terry Goodman, for believing in and working so tirelessly on *Crossing*.

Manhattan's Chinatown community that meant and continues to mean so much to me: Jeffrey He, Barry Li, Edward Tay, James Suen, Raymond Hom, Simon Wu, Yoki Poon, Ching-Hua Liang, Ken Tsui, Ricky Li, Gary Kwok, Will Liu, and Joanna Yip. Without you, I could never have written this novel. In particular: May Lee, Kenny Chau, Peter Ong, Marion Hsieh, Courtney Chinn, and Kyle Hubers.

My parents, who lovingly and wisely instilled in me a deep love for books; and my brothers, Jim and Mike, who encouraged me from an early age—by way of sibling rivalry—to write stories, stories, and more stories. This novel is the result.

My two energetic sons, Chris and John, who although too young to even read these words, have added balance, joy, and depth to both my life and writing.

And, most of all, Ching-Lee.

XING

- 星, pronounced *Shing*, meaning "star"
- a crossing

★

In the heady days of that winter, my name and face were plastered on the front page of every major newspaper and weekly newsmagazine. It was some years ago, I know, and many more sensational stories have come and gone, but perhaps you might recall the story if I remind you of some of the more salient details.

Do you remember my name, Xing Xu?

Or the newspaper photograph of me—that unflattering shot of me in my eighth grade class portrait where my head was circled to stand me out in the back row? I was frowning because of the harsh light, and my face looked pinched and stingy. There was no need to circle my head—I already stood out for obvious reasons.

Is it coming back to you yet? The Chinese kid who lived in an all-white town, attended an all-white high school, the shy outsider, aloof and inscrutable? The media even dug up my (fake) immigration papers, of all things. They left no stone unturned; but really, can you blame them? The public's hunger for information proved to be insatiable. *USA Today* published my report card, something I have mixed feelings about. It was nice for people to know about my A in English, but I wish I could have explained my C- in American History.

Surely you must remember by now. The kid who could sing like an angel? Or how about this, the ultimate buzzwords: *disappeared children*. That's what usually does it for most people, what triggers their memories. Just say "the disappeared children of Ashland, New York," and instantly they're thinking of me, that Chinese kid.

Articles, books, and even a made-for-TV movie special have depicted the events of that autumn. They tend to focus on the disappeared children. I wish they didn't do that. The story isn't really about them. And they always seem to start with the first disappearance, Justin Dorsey. See, right there and then, they have it all wrong. Because the story doesn't start with Dorsey. It doesn't start with any kind of disappearance. It starts, rather, with an appearance—the first appearance of that new girl during one of the snowiest autumns on record.

But they just don't understand that. They've never been able to.

AUGUST 27, 2008

In the fall of 2008, before the abductions began, I was a nervous freshman enrolled at Slackenkill High School. Five hundred and eighty-two students were officially enrolled, of whom I had significant interaction with only one: Naomi Lee. She was the only other Asian in the whole school. Yes, we stood out like sore thumbs. I'll spare you the clichés.

On the first day, I entered high school full of good intentions to make my social life a little more robust than my disastrous junior high school days. But to my dismay, I found—even on the very first day—that impenetrable cliques had already formed. Girls decked out in their pink spaghetti-strap blouses clamored into each other's tanned arms. Guys gave each other high-five fists. It was as if school had actually begun two weeks ago, and I, the latecomer, was arriving when the wet cement of social dynamics had already solidified.

Really, all I wanted on my first day of high school was to fly under the radar. Not an easy task, however, considering I was one of only two Asian students in an all-white school. And an almost impossible task when the homeroom teacher butchers your name beyond recognition.

"Ex-ing X-you?" she said. Her name was Miss Winters, and I took an instant dislike to her. She was a rotund woman with gobs of fat wobbling all over her body like Jell-O. For a teacher with years of experience, she seemed remarkably nervous that first day. She spoke in a pitched, shaky voice, bags of cheek fat quivering like they were trying to break free. When she had earlier written her name on the blackboard, her beefy hands swallowed up the piece of chalk, and the fat along the axis of her arm had swung like heavy pendulums.

The classroom, full of Smiths and Robinsons and Bernsteins, paused.

"Ex-ing X-you?" she asked again.

I raised my hand quickly. "Here," I mumbled.

Miss Winters stared at me over the top of her glasses. She moved her finger down to the next name, paused, then looked at me again. "How do you pronounce your name?" she asked through a shiny, plastic smile. She thought of herself as cultured, a world-traveling sophisticate.

"Call me Kris."

"But your Chinese name. How do you pronounce your Chinese name?"

"Just call me Kris."

She glanced down at the name again. "Ex-ing X-Sue?"

"Xing Xu," I said slowly, painfully. "But just call me Kris. *Please.*"

At this, the class burst out. My high school career was off to a rollicking start.

Only one other person was not laughing. My best—and only—friend, Naomi Lee, who was sitting next to me. Years ago, when she'd first arrived in my classroom fresh off the boat, I hated her. This "Oriental" girl—with her chop-suey English and FOB clothes—had brought unnecessary attention to all that differentiated me from my classmates, the kind of attention I'd spent years trying to avoid. But now I envied her. There was the simplicity of her name, for one. An official American first name that her parents had the wherewithal to give her when they first arrived. Plus the incredible fortune of having a Chinese surname that coincided with an American one.

But it was not only her name I secretly envied. She now spoke English with a pitch-perfect accent. I'd been in America two years longer than she, in fact, but you wouldn't know it from the heavily accented Chinglish I used. Her English was Julie Chen perfect; mine was Jackie Chan cumbersome. She had picked up English the way she picked up most everything else: quickly, brilliantly, naturally. She was an academic marvel, achieving in three years what few do in a lifetime. She had surpassed her white peers in every department, including English. She took sample SATs for fun and near aced them every time. She was destined for Harvard.

Just as the laughter was dying down, the principal, Mr. Marsworth, walked in. He was invariably a bungling mess. He could never get his hair in order, and his eyes, bugging out from the sockets, only added to his jittery aura. Behind him was a rather peculiar-looking girl.

The principal handed the girl over to Miss Winters, whispered a few quick words, and took off quickly, as if glad to unburden himself from a most disagreeable task. Miss Winters regarded the girl coolly.

"Class," she said in her shrill, officious voice, "let me interrupt you. Today we have a new student with us. Now, I know that we're all new students today, but she's especially new. She's from out of state, Montana. I'm sure all of us will extend to her the utmost of courtesy and warmth." She turned and prodded the girl forward. "OK, please introduce yourself to the class."

The girl stepped forward. Her skin was pale, melted candle wax flung onto bones. Her hair lay limp and lifeless in a matted mess. Her clothes hung on her like a reluctant after-thought.

The classroom waited in a silent mix of amusement and bemusement. The girl said nothing. Looking at her, I came away with the distinct impression of a passionless being, completely devoid of whatever it was that separated human beings from cardboard boxes.

"Just tell us your name and where you're from," Miss Winters urged.

Still she said nothing. She only stood in silence, hands trembling at her sides. Only then did I notice her thick eyebrows and piercing green eyes; against her pale face, they were startling in their intensity.

"No need to be afraid, now. Just tell us your name."

The girl hesitated like a child on a springboard. She murmured something, a whittled whisper.

"Speak louder," rang out Miss Winters.

"Jan Blair," the girl said.

"Blair?" asked Miss Winters. "Like the movie?"

The girl turned crimson. She nodded fiercely, but Miss Winters did not seem to understand.

"You know the movie," continued Miss Winters. *"The Blair Witch Project?"*

Jan Blair must have known it was inevitable. But even in her most pessimistic of moods, she'd likely never suspected it would have taken hold so quickly. And to be instigated by a teacher, at that.

"She's the Blair Witch!" someone yelled from the back of the classroom, and a heckler's chorus of jeers broke out. Miss Winters pressed a chubby finger against her lips, her shushing sound drowned out.

Jan Blair's head hung dejectedly as if her neck muscles had suddenly snapped. Her mangy bangs dangled over her face.

"The Blair Witch!" someone shouted again, relishing the moment.

"Be quiet!" shushed Miss Winters. "Quiet! Quiet," she said, flapping her arms uselessly like a hen. Around her, the ruckus only grew louder.

And then Jan Blair lifted her head. Only a little, just enough for her eyes to peer out from under her bangs. And perhaps her eyes just happened to find mine all the way in the back of the classroom, but it seemed as if she'd met them deliberately. Our gazes locked dead-on. For an awful moment, there was something like recognition...but then I flicked my eyes quickly away.

"The Blair Witch!" I shouted. Only Naomi seemed to notice next to me; she jolted a little in her seat. "The Blair Witch!" I shouted again, the volume and venom in my voice surprising even me.

———— ★ ————

For a few hours, the Blair Witch was the *it* thing to talk about. But interest proved to be short-lived, and by day's end she was mostly forgotten. There were other, more pressing things to talk about, such as who was the best kisser in school, whether Clarice David had gotten a nose job over the summer, and the like.

And because of something that later happened, Jan Blair became the last thing on my mind as well.

Naomi and I had agreed to meet at the library after school. When I got there, it was deserted—even the librarian was gone. I sat down with a newspaper in the periodicals section.

A gust of cold air rushed in, signaling the arrival of Naomi. Only it wasn't Naomi; the voices that flew in were coarse and choppy.

I never looked up from the paper. But I was no longer reading it; instead, using my peripheral vision, I kept tabs on the three boys who had just ambled in. They went to a nearby table, horsing around. By now they must have noticed me; if not, it was only a matter of time. They ripped pages out of magazines, crumpling them into paper balls, and shot them into a wastebasket located just at the foot of the circulation desk. They shuffled over to a stack of flyers. "Auditions for *The Man from Jerusalem* will begin the week of September 8," each flyer announced. The boys crumpled these into balls. They seemed preoccupied, and I rose from my chair and picked up my bag. Naomi was to meet me soon, and I wanted to leave before she walked in.

I was almost at the door when my foot banged against a trashcan. It was all too quiet suddenly, and as I reached for the doorknob, a paper ball hit me on the back of my head. Instantly there was an outburst of laughter from behind me. I turned.

It was my first good look at the boys, and nothing about them surprised me. I'd seen their kind a hundred times before. One of them, Trey Logan, was the leader of the gang. I already knew his reputation: a louse who'd once knocked his third grade teacher unconscious with a baseball bat. He was a skinny stick who always wore oversized Wal-Mart clothes. A scuttle of angry red zits lay scattered across his pointy chin. A Mount St. Helens of a pimple was lodged under his right nostril, at least three days overripe.

Logan did not know this yet—no one knew this—but in a few months he would be dead. His name and face would be splashed all over the Internet and newspapers. But he could not possibly have known this now.

"Hey, it's Jet Li!" Laughter. They were spreading across the room slowly, casting a wider net around me. I could see that they were experienced; they knew their trade, and they were good at what they did. Their next move would be to try to cut me off from the door. But I was also good at what I'd been forced to learn over the years—the art of evasion

"Hey," Trey said. His voice was almost kind, that of a grandmotherly librarian. "You forgot to put away the newspaper. It's the rule."

All three had moved away from that table. There seemed to be no danger in simply walking back to the newspaper. But I didn't bite. They'd wait until I reached the paper, and the second I did, they'd move swiftly, as one, not towards me but to the door to barricade it with their bodies. Then I would be trapped. Then they would pounce.

I looked at each boy in turn: they meant to do damage. It was marked in their eyes and slightly crooked elbows.

"Aww, look," Logan said with false sympathy. "He doesn't speak. Just like that Virginia Tech killer. Quiet and all." He leered at me, looking at my bag. "What you got in there? Guns? You're gonna try to cut us down, just like that Virginia Tech guy?"

I could still walk out the door if I wanted to. Forget what happened. Try to.

"You forgot to pick up your paper balls," I said, pointing to the cluster lying at the foot of the trashcan in the corner. "You missed all your shots." Their faces were momentary portraits of surprise. "Pick them up. It's the rule."

They were stumped. These were boys who lacked the intelligence to make a witty verbal comeback; all they knew about retaliation was the fisticuffs kind. They'd expected my Asian tail to tuck between my legs, a submissive china doll to beat up on. They looked at me for a few seconds, then at each other, momentarily confused.

"What did he say?" said the shorter boy. "Was that English?"

"'Ching chong cha chink chong ah so,' is what he said," replied the other.

I spoke again, trying to sound assertive, my voice quivering a little. "Don't throw paper balls at me."

"*Don't throw paper balls at me*,'" Logan mocked in a falsetto impersonation. "Please don't bruise my pretty yellow skin with a paper ball," he continued. "Me no see ball through my squinty little eyes." He pulled his arm back and threw another paper ball at me.

The ball whizzed past my head, missing my right ear by about ten feet.

"Please tell me you weren't aiming for me," I said. The words, decent enough, I suppose, nonetheless quivered in my eggshell voice.

The three boys began to move in. As they did, something began to wilt in me. Now would be the time to bolt out the door.

But I did not. Years back, in elementary school when the bullying had first begun, I had forced myself never to run, never to cower. Initially, it had been hard, and I'd still ended up running away in tears. But I learned to buoy myself up, to stanch the need to bolt. But all that anger was inflicted on me. Then internalized. I used to wonder about all that anger, where it all went. You can only take in so much. Somehow it has to come out, find release.

The boys edged closer to me now. I dropped my bag to the ground.

At the very second God created me, He must have blinked. And ever since, He's been blinking a lot; every time something like this happens to me, I'm in one of His blinks.

I'm glad it was the librarian who walked in minutes later and not Naomi. She should never see what the librarian witnessed when she opened the door. Chairs overturned, tables pushed haphazardly to the side, books pulled off shelves onto the floor. Three boys, shirts disheveled, their hair ruffled, their anger unhinged, atop another whose face was hidden, pinned down. Again and again, fists raining down on him. One of them, Trey Logan, on top and straddling me, rabid with a tunnel-vision anger. "What kind of a Jet Li are you?" he yelled, his face beet red. "What the hell kind of a Jet Li are you?"

Naomi and I walked home in somber silence. The sky, spread above in a velvet expanse, darkened like a bloodying blister. Naomi occasionally glanced sideways at me. My wounds were mostly superficial, the nurse had said, and I was fortunate to not be any worse off. I was lucky, Mr. Marsworth had concurred from where he stood looking out the window, lucky I wasn't hurt any worse. Those three were very bad boys. Mandatory Saturday detentions, he said, at least four weeks. He nodded his head as he said this, a rooster pulling at its wattle chin.

Truth is, they had no idea how bad it was for me. Under my clothes, my body was a hodgepodge of discolored patches of blue and purple. Every time I took a step and my backpack jiggled against my back, I felt a raw rub of pain sear up and down. My only consolation was *The Punch*—a solid connection that had landed square on Logan's eyeball. I'd felt the taut liquid bulge of his eye give under my fist, felt his bony eye socket crack under my knuckles. Within minutes after *The Punch*, a huge welt had formed under his quickly blackening eye.

And one other thing: sometime during the melee, I made *The Grab*. It happened as I'd reached up to scratch his eyes out—I didn't have a whole lot of options. But instead of finding his eyes, my fingers sank into his neck, hooking around a gold chain. I didn't even remember ripping it off, but afterwards on my way to the infirmary I felt it snaked around my wrist. I slipped it into my rear jeans pocket. No way I was going to give it back to Logan. So between *The Punch* and *The Grab*, I didn't think I'd made out so bad.

"Does it hurt when I do this?" Naomi suddenly asked, and just as suddenly she whipped back her arm and slap-punched me.

"Ouch! What the hell did you do that for?"

"So it does hurt!" she exclaimed, almost jubilant that her suspicions were confirmed.

"Well, I got hit, Naomi! I got gang-attacked. Of course it's gonna hurt." I rubbed my smarting arm. "They got punches in on me, you know."

"Well, no, I don't know, because somebody isn't talking."

"That's only because…" I began, then I let my words drift into a sullen silence.

"You should have told me," she said in a voice suddenly tender. We walked with the echo of those words strung between us. A flock of birds took off from a tree, stripping it of its fullness. They meandered indecisively before flying east, toward the hills. "How bad is it?" she asked softly.

I didn't want to tell her the truth. I kept walking.

"I know you're hurting," she said. "You never carry your bag over your left shoulder. Your strides are usually longer, and you're walking much slower. Xing, listen to me!" She stopped walking, forcing me to stop and turn to her.

"I'm all right, OK?"

But she was shaking her head. "What are you going to do?"

"What do you mean, 'What are you going to do?'"

"Logan isn't going to forget this. He's gonna exact revenge."

I started to walk. "I don't think so. He'll just let it go."

"No way. That black eye you gave him is going to be a daily reminder to him of his utter humiliation. Every time he looks in the mirror and sees a black-eyed panda staring back, he's gonna get stewed. You're a marked man, Xing, you need to know that."

"I wouldn't worry," I said, chest puffed out. "I've already proven I can take care of myself."

She looked skeptical. "Someone like Logan will hold a grudge against you for months."

She was right, but there was really nothing to be done. In a few weeks, if not days, Logan was going to drop me. It might be anywhere: in the cafeteria, in an empty bathroom at school, on the school bus. Somewhere, it was almost guaranteed, I was going to be felled with a punch to the stomach, a kick to the groin, a knuckle to the head. Logan would make sure I was physically marked this time—two black eyes, a few missing teeth, maybe even a slit earlobe. Anything to put the world on notice that he wasn't going to take nothing from no one.

"I'll be careful," I said. It sounded unconvincing even in my own ears.

We reached the M15 bus stop for Ashland Mall. "Coming?" Naomi asked.

"Not today," I answered. "Got some things I need to do."

She stared at me for a second or two. "Try to take a hot bath," she said. "If you start to swell in places, apply some ice. If you can, try to get a few aspirins for the pain. Ibuprofens if you have them at home. For the swelling."

I waited with her for the bus. The frigid air seemed ready to crackle and splinter. At one point, Naomi took out her winter hat. She tilted her head back, angling it at a slant so that her long hair fell straight down. With a quick swing of her head, she swished the hat on perfectly, her hair neatly caught and held under. She smiled at me, satisfied.

When the bus arrived, she waved a quick good-bye before stepping on. It lurched forward with a groan. Her routine was the same every day—after school, she took this bus to the mall and made her way to the food court. Her parents worked in the Panda House, slaving away in the small confines, the smell of kung pao chicken, spicy cashew chicken, and spring rolls seeping into their clothes, their hair, the deep grooves of their forehead wrinkles. Naomi stayed there every night, studying at one of the tables in the food court, her textbooks splayed about her. When things got busy, she sixth-sensed her parents' need and made her way around the counter to help out until the swell of customers subsided. Then she'd get back to her books, picking up exactly where she'd left off.

When she first immigrated to America years ago, I'd been forced to tutor her, to help her with homework in the food court. Even back then, as peeved as I was having to teach— having to merely *associate* with—this little Chinese girl who spoke no English, I'd been amazed at her powers of concentration, the knitted brow, the tilted head. Only three years passed before the tables were turned, when the student not only surpassed the teacher but became the teacher.

I watched her bus turn the corner before I trudged home alone. But I had something. When she'd pulled on her wool hat, a faint whiff of her shampoo entered my nose. The fragrance would linger, seemingly for hours. All I had to do in the endless stretch of hours in my room was to inhale deeply, and I would smell the meadow fragrance—fainter with each passing hour but, I'd think, still there.

If you've never been inside a cold, dark abyss of gloom, then you'd have a hard time picturing my home. It was the only home I'd ever had in America, a ramshackle house surely in violation of at least a dozen housing codes. The heating was touch and go; there was a constant cold draft snaking through the house, and the pipes clicked and rattled constantly. It was always dark inside. This I never understood. It could have been Dante's *Inferno* bright outside, but it'd still be dark inside, as if rays of light just wilted on contact with the walls and windows of this house. I'd be tempted to say this house was like a rusted-over empty birdcage, but that wouldn't be true. This house had actual occupants. This bare, cold, sullen house. And ever since my father died, all the barer and colder.

I made my way up the staircase, each step creaking in time with my aching body. Into the dank bathroom, where I turned on the light switch. A sickly yellow fluorescent light urinated down on me. In the mirror, I saw blandness, the kind of face passed over in a crowd, the plainness of features that could drive a caricaturist out of business. My blah face, tight nose, earthworm lips, thin eyes (yes, OK, they were squinty, shut up already)—an impenetrable mask to all around. Years ago, I used to play with my features in this mirror, using my fingers to push down the angled tilt of the corner of my eyes, and picture myself with blond hair and blue eyes. In those moments, I fantasized that deep within me was a white boy on the fringe of freeing himself from the constricting bamboo chains. That one day my eyes would downturn themselves, ovalize, even turn blue.

The same eyes stared back at me now. Anger had taken root in them, festering over the years. They were darker now, cold as marbles. There were days I did not recognize them.

After a long shower, I sat on the edge of the bath basin, suddenly weak with fatigue. I hadn't eaten much all day, and wave upon wave of hunger crashed upon me. And then, the smell of food. It wafted up from the kitchen downstairs, thick and luxurious, succulence slipping through the floorboards. I opened the door and stood cautiously. The sound of pots and pans clanging, of plates being set on the table.

An elderly woman was standing by the stove when I entered the kitchen, a threadbare cooking apron tied around her thin waist, tight as a straitjacket. It was Miss Durgenhoff, a boarder who'd arrived in nondescript fashion a few weeks ago. She'd settled in very quietly in the room next to mine, keeping mostly to herself, silent as a bat; she was the perfect unobtrusive tenant who settled into place without fanfare. After my father's death, money had become especially tight; my mother started renting out what had been his painting studio to tenants. Most were usually gone within a few months, loners, misplaced transients between nowhere and nowhere. Miss Durgenhoff was likely the same.

She shuffled from stove to table, her gnarled hands cupping the handles of a pot, plumes of steam swirling upwards. The table was laden with a feast, a banquet, a buffet.

"Ahh," she said in a slightly phlegmy voice, "there you are." She quickly smiled at me before turning back to the stove. Her glasses steamed up with condensation, hiding her eyes. "Thought I'd cook tonight for a change. And look, enough to feed an army. Want some?"

"Like you wouldn't believe," I replied, and already she was piling food onto my plate. For the next few minutes, I ate ravenously. The food melted richly over my tongue, then seemed to explode in rapture. I couldn't seem to chew fast enough. Thick, oozing gravy draped itself over my tongue in a loving embrace, and when I swallowed, I felt the warm gravy hum all the way down to my stomach.

"It takes fifteen minutes for the stomach to tell you that it's full." She chuckled to herself. "You should stop eating for a while. Soon your stomach will go from telling you it's empty to telling you it's on the verge of exploding."

"This food," I said, chewing, "hits the spot just so." I took a gulp from a pinkish fruit juice.

"I take it your mother doesn't cook very often."

"She comes home too late." *And I don't have to eat and sit with her afterward*, I thought but did not say.

"What do you do for dinner, then?"

"Oh," I said, reaching for another helping of meatloaf, "I eat with my friend, Naomi, sometimes. Her parents work at the food court at a mall nearby, and I mooch off of them. I bring back food for those nights when I just eat here. Chinese food tastes good leftover, too."

She *tsked tsked* me and shuffled over to the stove, where she filled a bowl with soup and brought it to me. "Have some of this; it's good for you. It'll help with the bruising."

I kept on chewing, hiding my surprise. "How did you know I have bruises?"

"You live up to my age, and you learn to see past the surface stuff." She saw the confusion on my face. "It's the way you're sitting, how you seem to be favoring different body postures. What was it, football practice?"

"No, I just fell down the steps."

She shook her head. "You young people," she said ambiguously, but her eyes were clear. She knew. After a moment, she smiled. "Come now," she said, "the soup's best when piping hot."

The soup was a bitter concoction of what appeared to be chicken legs, sticky rice, hard radish, bamboo shoots, sweet potatoes, butternut squash, and an unidentifiable spicy substance that serrated against my tongue like a splintered ruler.

"How is it?"

"It tastes like medicine."

"Thank you," she said. "Its medicinal side effects are quite renowned, to say nothing of its flavor."

"So how long are you planning on staying here, Miss Durgenhoff?" I asked, putting the spoon down, completely satisfied.

She leaned back against the back of the chair. Her eyes stared out, moist with fatigue. She sighed and stood up slowly, her arms pushing up on the table. "Oooh. I fear I've been stationary for too long. Can't let that happen at my age."

"Let me help clean up."

"No, no, I won't have it. You'll just get in the way. Go upstairs and do your homework."

"I should help."

"No, no. Just leave me be."

I was almost out the kitchen when she asked me a question. A curious question.

"Do you know where the boy lives?"

"What boy?"

"The boy who hit you."

She was washing the dishes, her back to me. She never stopped washing, never turned around.

"No, I—"

"OK, good night, Kris."

I studied her for a few seconds, the steam from the hot water filling the room, clouding my vision. She disappeared in that gathering steam.

In the middle of the night, I awoke. I lay staring at the night outside, thinking, as I often did in bed, of my hometown in China. It was daytime there now: the streets overflowing with teeming crowds, the flow of bicycles, the honking of cars, the sun hot and smoldering. Children leaving school, chasing each other in the streets, stopping at a cart to buy a slice of watermelon from a hawker. I could see myself, the me that never left China. Always surrounded by friends, always laughing with abandon, always with a twinkle of confidence in my eyes. My skin a deep bronze from the burning sun, my hair tousled lightly in the warm breeze. I am smiling as I run home, shouting my farewells to friends, my voice unhinged in exuberance, unbridled in its own sureness. I am rushing home to the wondrous smells of home cooking, to the warm greetings of my mother, grandmother, of my father…

I pushed the blankets aside and stood at the window. Our car—husk-like under the garage light—sat in the driveway. I had not heard my mother return. Ever since my father's death, she worked two jobs: at a massage parlor in a tiny strip mall during the day, and as a hospital janitor at night. She never spoke of her jobs. It wasn't usually until past midnight that she returned; she no longer minded the fact that I was already in bed. We barely saw each other anymore, and we spoke even less, only on Sunday nights, and it was always the same damn thing. "Have you done all your homework?" she'd ask me, and then without waiting for an answer she'd monotone, "Education is everything." Every Sunday night. Without fail.

Looking at my clothes lying discarded on the floor, I remembered something. I picked up my jeans and fished out Trey Logan's gold chain that I'd snatched during the fight. On a small plate between links, the initials *TL* glimmered in the moonlight. There was a place for this, I decided. Taking down a painting from my wall, I located a wood panel in the wall. It was a small, L-shaped panel indistinguishable from its surroundings. I jarred it loose with my fingernails, as I had done countless times before. From behind the panel I removed a small pouch. It contained a slew of coins and petty cash I had picked up over the years. My "getaway" money. I threw Logan's gold chain into the pouch.

I was about to go back to bed when I saw someone standing across the street. A dark shadow, stationary, barely noticeable. A flash of red color. Then it retreated into the shadows and whisked away so quickly that I wondered if I'd imagined the whole thing.

NIGHT

*I*t isn't the first time Justin Dorsey has snuck out at night to meet Susan, but it is the first time she stands him up.

Every night for the past two weeks he has met her by the lake. She is always there first, eyes shimmering with anticipation, her hair freshly shampooed and smelling nice. And she can always be counted on to bring everything: the snacks, the drinks, the blankets. He understands her excitement. He's a catch, a high school sports stud and academic star, and her stock will only rise if word gets out.

Justin intends to keep these trysts a secret. He can do so much better than Susan, truth be told, but she's just a quick filler for him while his girlfriend is away in Paris on a high school exchange program. He has needs, after all, an overpowering urge that surprises even him at times.

If you love me, you'll keep this a secret. *That's what he'd planned to tell Susan tonight. Except she's a no show. He waits fifteen minutes before heading back, miffed.*

Well, *he thinks to himself as he walks back*, there's a first time for everything in life.

Another first is awaiting him that night.

He can hardly have known this as he approaches the walkover. He hates this walkover, filthy as it is, but he has to take it every time. It's the only way to cross Route 82. It is nothing but a thin strip of corru-

gated metal and tired concrete arching over the highway, mostly forgotten, barely used.

And filthy. Discarded trash strewn amok. Empty beer bottles cast to the side. A layer of soot and grime coats the walkover, years of accumulated car exhaust. Dark. Whatever lamps once illuminated it, their bulbs have long since burned out.

The place stinks of urine and wet cigarette butts and spilled beer.

Traffic is sparse underneath him even for that time of night. A few solitary flecks of light in the distance. He pauses in the middle of the walkover, seeing something down at his feet.

Now that, he thinks to himself, is disgusting.

There's a dead cat lying there. He almost stepped on it in the darkness.

Because he is so focused on the cat, he doesn't notice the dark figure climbing the stairs behind him.

Justin stoops lower to take a closer look. The cat has bled from the head, profusely. This isn't a natural death, not with these injuries. More like roadkill. Only...how has the cat ended up here?

And something else. The cat wasn't here when he crossed over just twenty minutes prior. He sniffs, doesn't smell rot or decay.

Shards of glass being stepped on. From behind him. He spins around.

"I'm sorry, I didn't mean to startle you." The face so close, Justin can see little specks of saliva on the wet, blubbering lips.

"Well, you did, damn it."

"I'm sorry."

There shouldn't be anything to be afraid of. Not of this person anyway, a person who should be more afraid of him, really. But for some unfathomable reason, Justin is afraid.

As if reading his mind, the person says, "Don't be afraid."

"I'm not."

"Don't be scared."

"I keep telling you I'm not."

"Scaredy cat."

"Excuse me?"

"Scaredy cat. That's what you are."

Justin takes a step backwards. *"Look, why don't you just—"*

"Meow. Meow. Just like this scared little cat. It went meow, meow. You're just like this cat. Meow."

Justin doesn't respond. On the football field he has faced down towering opponents, hulking masses of brute strength. He has dealt with much worse than the lithe figure in front of him. But there is something nakedly off-kilter about this person, disconcertingly askew. Justin backpedals on suddenly wobbly legs.

"Oh," and there is genuine pity on the face, *"are you trying to get away?"*

And it is that pity, so sincere and sure of itself, that causes Justin to turn and run.

"You can try *to get away,"* Justin hears from behind him, *"just like this cat did."*

For the first time in his life, Justin feels raw horror. And then he feels a blackness, a coldness, then nothing at all.

SEPTEMBER 10

It was Mr. Brooks, the school janitor for over three decades, who came across the frozen corpse. It was early in the morning, barely past dawn, when he noticed a mysterious, dark lump at the flagpole. He headed over. At first, he thought it was all a prank. Some jokesters had planted a mannequin; they were probably filming him from some secret spot, hoping to embarrass him on YouTube. But as he drew closer, his steps slowed first with uncertainty then with dawning horror. The body was too real, and the face was suddenly too recognizable. It was the face of Justin Dorsey, encrusted with ice, ashen and ghostlike. Within ten minutes, police cars were shrieking onto school grounds.

Only a few students saw the body. Sensitive to the effect a corpse would have on high schoolers, police rushed their on-scene operations. What should have taken at least five hours to complete was wrapped up in under two. By the time the majority of students arrived at school, the stiffened body had long since been whisked away. Only a few police officers milled around, keeping at bay a growing mass of reporters.

Word of what happened whipped around school in a frenzy. Students huddled in groups to gossip or gabbed away on their cell phones. A few fainted; others could be seen trembling with tear-streaked faces, inconsolable. Counselors were quickly brought in. Some parents came by to pick up their reluctant—and somewhat embarrassed—children. No one knew why the principal didn't cancel school.

I eavesdropped as much as possible in the hallways and corridors. Most of it was wild speculation: Dorsey was decapitated; he was strangled; there were knife wounds on him; he had committed suicide. It was impossible to separate truth from fiction. I wanted to find Naomi to see what she knew, but in the chaos of the day she was impossible to find.

So I walked around aimlessly, meandering along the eastern wing, a secluded area of school. I was halfway down the corridor on the second floor when I made a disconcerting discovery: Trey Logan. He had just walked out of a restroom, still zipping his fly, directly in front of me. His zipper was jammed, so his attention was temporarily distracted. His bruised eye was a hazy smear of spilled ink, fainter now. Voices emanated from the restroom, leering sneers uncomfortably familiar. I froze with indecision. If I just stood perfectly stationary, maybe he wouldn't see me, maybe I would blend into my surroundings, maybe

I knew better.

I reached for a doorknob to my left, keeping my eyes trained on Logan. Through just a crack, I—ghostlike—slipped through. I closed the door quickly, quietly, ear pressed against the door, foot jammed rigid against the bottom of the door. It never occurred to me to look behind me.

"Can I help you?" said an impatient voice from inside the classroom.

I spun around. I was in the music room, a large, spare room entombed by the dreary faces of dead composers hung within dusty frames on all walls. A grand piano stood in the dead center of the room; next to it, stern and pale, was

Mr. Theodore Matthewman, the music teacher. His demeanor was identical to the portraits around him, as if he'd just stepped out of one himself.

"Well, speak up, boy!" His voice was a raspy collection of phlegm.

I fidgeted, tugged at my left sleeve.

"What! Lost your tongue, boy?" He glared at me. "Do you even speak English?"

I briefly thought of easing the door open just a crack to see if Logan had moved on. But I heard voices—no more than a mere foot or two on the other side—jocular and berating. So this was my dilemma: in front of me, the cantankerous and crotchety Mr. Matthewman; behind me, the voices of gang-terrorism. I chose the lesser of two evils.

"I...came...in...here..." I stammered, having no idea of what I was going to say next.

He leaned forward as if on an invisible cane. His face pinched like an imploding papier-mâché. "Get out! You're wasting my time!"

I could still hear the voices. "I came in...to...try...try..."

His eyes suddenly widened, naked with ridicule. "For the tryout? To audition?" He pushed his glasses up higher on the bridge of his nose. "To audition? *You?*" His craggy eyes moved up and down my person, incredulous. "Well, speak up!"

Mr. Matthewman carried with him a reputation of being a piano maestro long past his heyday, a man whose considerable gifts were never fully realized because of some scandal when he was a professor at Julliard. Now he was only a shell of the man he'd once been, full of sour spit and rancid breath.

"Here for the audition?" His voice was still incredulous. "Speak up or get out of here."

And before I really knew what I was saying, I heard myself say, "Yes. Here for *The Man from Bethlehem.*"

"Jerusalem!" he barked at me. "At least get the name straight." His eyes seared through me as he walked slowly back to the piano, muttering. He thumbed his way through a stack of music sheets. "You know that the lead position has already been filled?"

"Yes." In fact, everyone knew. The name Anthony Hasbourd had become synonymous with Lead Singer in School Production. He was a mediocre singer whose parents had the misbegotten idea that he was the next Josh Groban. He flaunted and preened every year on stage, conveniently forgetting that he had "won" the lead only because his parents financed the productions. So nobody bothered to audition against him since it was simply assumed the role belonged to him.

Matthewman squinted his eyes at me, shriveling me down. "Are you sure you want to audition?" He waited, his body hunched over.

I didn't say anything; he coughed into his hands, then flung his arm out. A sheet of music hung on the end of it, stiff and crinkly. I took it, staring dumbly at it.

"Very well, then. Let's do this." His fingers touched the keyboard and began to play. His eyes were fixed on me. He was curious.

It had been many years since I last sang. There was a time, back in my village in China, when I sang all the time. Whole days spent fishing with my father on the Chengzi River, my voice rising with the dawn sun; then through the hot afternoon, in cadence with the lazy sound of water lapping against the wood boat. Mine was a beautiful voice, so my father used to tell me, as mesmerizing as a thousand shooting stars. And my parents wanted me to sing all the time,

I remember, especially in the hot summer nights when the town lost electricity and the small bedroom fan stood limp and useless. *Sing us to sleep, Xing*, they pleaded. *Help us forget the heat*. And I would sing soft lullabies in the dark until they stopped wiping sweat from their brows and kicking at invisible blankets at their feet. Sandwiched between them, feeling their body heat humming against me, I never felt safer, never felt calmer, than when I sang into the night even after they had fallen asleep. But after I arrived on the shores of America, I did not sing very much. Something seemed to lodge itself into my throat, inhibiting me. In the cacophony of foreign sounds flooding my ears, I lost my ability to speak, much less sing. I became quiet; I diminished. Over time, I sang less and less, until all those songs I'd once cherished disappeared somewhere within me. And one day I stopped singing altogether.

Mr. Matthewman's eyes blazed into me, as if daring me. His fingers danced gracefully across the keyboard like a separate animal.

I stared down at the notes in my hands. They looked as foreign to me as English words once had. I stood very, very still. The stillness of the clueless.

And when the moment came, I made as gallant an effort as I could.

There are a number of ways to describe the noise that scraped out of my voice box. A pigeon's beak scratched across the blackboard, a shard of glass scraped against a rusty pipe, a fork dragged hard against a car's iced-over windscreen. Mr. Matthewman's face said it all, a look of surprised agony.

"What in…?"

I held up my hand pathetically. "I'm sorry, Mr. Matthewman. I…I think I can do better." I looked down at the music sheets. "Please, sir, I think I can do better."

"Is this some sick joke?" His eyes were smoldering pieces of coal. "Get out!"

"Please, Mr. Matthewman!" It was the loudest I'd ever spoken to a teacher. "Give me just one last shot."

There must have been something in my voice, some look in my face, because he did just that. He gave me one last chance.

But when I opened my mouth to sing, out came the pigeon's beak, the glass shard, the fork. All came tumbling out.

Trey Logan and his gang were gone by the time I walked out of the music room, not that I cared anymore. I felt strangely discombobulated. It wasn't until I splashed water on my face in the restroom that I was able to put a label to my knotted feelings.

I was angry at my failure.

The audition was only a stupid thing I had to do. A cowardly way of escape in an unwelcoming burrow as I waited for predators to pass on by outside. Yet why was the crumpled paper still in my hand, why my refusal to throw it away?

I looked down at it. The notes were still nothing more than black ink marks. My hands crushed the sheet into a ball, crinkling it, the sound filling the hollow right angles of the tiled room.

I heard the soft piano notes in my mind. They were coming back to me, their gentle initial cadence. It was cold in the bathroom, but my insides were hot with frustration. The notes. I was hearing them now. The way I should have heard them. Not trying to match them up with the black ink on paper. I reached for the light switch and turned it off. Curtains of darkness fell all around me. Still not dark enough. I shut my eyes.

This was how I had sung during those two awful weeks when I crossed the seas to America. In total darkness. On a cargo ship, locked in with dozens of others in a container. It had been stifling hot in that tin can, suffocating; but what I remember most was not the heat but the darkness. An endless black night without moon, without stars, the allure of America almost lost in the stench of human perspiration, desperation, urine, and worse. Tired yet unable to sleep, my parents would ask me to sing, as they had on stifling summer nights before. I was happy to oblige. Timidly at first, afraid of the darkness, of the faceless voices barking and crying in the black void, I would whisper out a few lines. But they would quiet whenever I began to sing, until—but for the occasional cough or sneeze in the hot darkness—a hush would befall us. In that hush, I sang. And it was as if cool mountain breezes came upon us; as if river waters suddenly flowed over our toes; as if the graceful dusk sun splashed down on our uplifted faces.

"Sing 'Autumn Moon on the Calm Lake,'" they would request of me. "Sing 'The Glow of the Setting Sun on the Lei Fong Pagoda.' Now sing 'Orioles Singing in the Willows.'" Always I did. "Sing 'Snow on the Broken Bridge.' 'Evening Knell on the Nan Ping.' 'Viewing Fish in Huagang.'" And I did. Over and over. I never sang as beautifully as I did in those two weeks.

And now for the first time in years, I felt a trembling in me again. With one hand pressed against the cold, tiled wall, I sealed my eyes shut. I replayed the gentle cadence in my head, the prodding of piano notes. The pitch. And the cold of the restroom began to recede, the sound of notes sharpening.

Now, I told myself. *Now*.

A long-lost voice sprang out of me. The windows shook in astonishment.

And I sang. I felt the words arch up out of me like molten ore. All these years, bottled within, germinating, now finding release. The music vibrated in me, a jaunty horse restless to be released. I felt the cadence of the song, a flowing carpet that lifted me high. I harnessed my voice, nuanced out the slightest inflections of sounds. And when at last the final note trailed out into a stillness, I was breathless.

I opened my eyes. I saw the look of wonder on my face in the hazy mirror. I was shaking slightly from side to side. Trembling.

The door. Sometime during my singing, it had opened and I hadn't even noticed. There was someone standing there. He had one hand lifted in front of his gaping mouth like a shy geisha. Astonished. Bewildered. Stupefied.

Enchanted.

It was Mr. Matthewman.

SEPTEMBER 12

Y ou're not joking?" she asked.

It was a couple days later on a late Friday afternoon. Naomi and I sat in the mostly vacant food court, in that gap of time after housewives had left but before the hoards of Friday night revelers arrived. I'd been biding my time to tell her about the audition. I wanted to do it where it was quiet, and with all the pandemonium at school over the last few days, this was my first opportunity.

"You are. You are joking, right?" she said.

"No," I said for the second time, this time barely able to conceal my annoyance.

"I can't believe," she said, pulling her eyebrows together in a soft, irritating arch, "that Mr. Matthewman thinks you can take the lead role. I mean, I've heard you sing, Xing. I know what you sound like." She sent me a smile that I knew wasn't meant to be unkind.

"You've never heard me sing."

"My point exactly. In music class way back when, you just stood silent, you *hmm hmm hmm*-ed your way through class."

"But you've never really heard me sing. Mr. Matthewman thinks I'm good enough."

Her fingers drummed against the table. A few seconds lapsed. Then she took a deep breath. "Please don't take this the wrong way, OK, Xing? I'm sure you did really well at the audition and everything, but..."

I leaned back in my seat. "What? Just say it, will you?"

"It's no secret that Matthewman hates Anthony Hasbourd. Hates the fact that the school makes him coach Hasbourd every year for the school production. Hates the way Hasbourd's parents think their son is too good for him."

"I know. So what are you saying?"

"It's just that..." She looked at me. "Do you think he might be using you to get back at Hasbourd?"

I reached down and stuffed a spring roll into my mouth. I chewed slowly. "I'm not replacing Hasbourd. I'm only going to be his understudy. I just wanted you to know of the audition, that it went well."

"I'm sorry, Xing," she said, leaning forward towards me sincerely. "I didn't mean to say anything hurtful."

"You weren't there. How do you know what I sounded like?"

"I've known you my whole life, practically. I know what you sound like."

"But you weren't there when I auditioned. You have no idea what I can sound like." I took the last spring roll, the one I had been planning on leaving for her, and rammed it in. I chewed hard, vigorously. "It doesn't matter in any case," I said through a mouthful. "Hasbourd's still got the lead."

She looked at me and didn't say anything.

I chewed harder, swallowed. Sometimes I could just about kill her.

"What exactly did Matthewman say?"

"He thought I was amazing and told me so." I could still hear the words resonating in my ears. "He said I was raw but had real talent."

"I'm sorry, I just can't see it."

I picked up my cup and sipped through the straw, sucking up pockets of empty air. "He said he wants me to come in early every morning to practice. I don't know if I should or not. Probably not. I don't know."

The truth: I was confused. The thought that maybe it *was* just an aberrational fluke had crossed my mind a thousand times. Maybe it was just the acoustics of the bathroom or a once-in-a-billion, never-to-be-repeated freakish moment.

I wanted to switch topics, and quickly. I knew exactly what to do. Deep down, past the nice-girl act, Naomi believed the world revolved around her. Talk about her, and her eyes would illuminate, her head would become just that little more animated.

"Anyway, I was really nervous at the audition," I said. "What do you usually do to calm yourself down before singing? I mean, you're doing a duet at church tonight, right?"

"Well," she said, perking up. I had her. "It's important to keep yourself warm; drink a lot of warm fluids. Look," she said, pointing at her cup of Lipton tea, "see?" She swiped a few strands of hair that had come loose behind her ear. Two strands sashayed before her prominent cheekbones. "And the worst thing you can do is worry too much about it. Do something fun. Hang out with friends. Get your mind off it for a while. Look." She pointed at the two of us, her index finger swiveling around like a door opening and closing between us. "See?" And she smiled in that incandescent, winning way of hers.

I tried not to stare at her as she spoke. Her hair was fuller now, a lush fall of silkiness. And her baby fat had burned off to reveal soft cheekbones and a chin that was elegantly pointed. Dimples once hidden by her baby fat were now punctures of sweetness: when she smiled, I wanted to embed my fingertips in them. And her arms and legs had grown longer and leaner, too; what a marvel to watch her during gym class as she rose up in the air to spike the volleyball, her arms twirling in a menagerie in tandem with one another, working in unison with her springing legs, the rich upper thighs glimmering with the reflection of the fluorescent lamps above.

Her intelligence had already been noticed at school, that sprightly, coquettish mind. Her steely concentration was impressive, her luminescent eyes absorbing, digesting. She grabbed facts, pulled in concepts, owned them. She was already light-years ahead of teachers whose idea of intelligence was scoring a perfect ten on a spelling test composed of words like *bereavement, pedestrian,* and *monotonous.* She was meant for the stars, and they were measuring her with their plastic white Wal-Mart rulers.

Very soon boys at school would start taking notice. Attention was slow in the coming at a school where boys thought that *Charlie's Angels* starred Cameron Diaz, Drew Barrymore, and some Asian chick. But a girl the likes of Naomi did not go unnoticed for long.

So when she asked me if I wanted to go to church with her that night, a place I resented with every fiber of my being, my answer was a foregone conclusion.

Redeemer Church of Ashland was where all the successful in Ashland showed off their wares: their cars, their clothes, and most of all their children. Adolescents came decked out in their Limited, Banana Republic, and Abercrombie & Fitch designer clothes. They had their laptops, their digital cameras, and their iPhones. And incredible teeth. Pearly white, perfectly aligned. In the winter they all loved to wear black turtlenecks, and their teeth glimmered brilliantly above the black like a halo.

They spoke of things I never felt at ease with, GPAs and honor societies and Princeton Reviews and summer school at Phillips Exeter or Andover and spring break mission trips to Paris or Vienna. On rare occasions when I visited—really just to be with Naomi, though I never told her so—I steered clear of them as much as possible. I watched them during youth worship, playing on their pricey guitars and flutes and violins and cellos, some with their own cars sitting in the church parking lot, others with doting parents waiting to take them home to their five-bedroom cul-de-sac McMansions. During Bible study, they crinkled the pages of their leather-bound King James Version Bibles. They spoke of their sufferings and travails, all trivial. God was in the details of their suburban self-esteem.

They were the sumptuous feast of life. Me, the stingy, cold leftover.

It wasn't long before worship began. I seated myself in the back pew of the swank sanctuary, removed from the others. Naomi made her way to the stage.

She stood alone at first, waiting for her duet partner to make his way to the stage. For a few moments, every eye was upon her, glowing and vulnerable in that soft light; yet, in her stillness, she was assured and certain. Something in me began to unravel. I wanted to lay my hand on her neck in the soft crevice just under her jawline.

Then somebody stood up and started to make his way to the stage. Anthony Hasbourd. I should have known. Of course it would be Hasbourd, that pretentious snob.

I closed my eyes.

At first, it was only Naomi's voice. Tender, as if she were right next to me, her mouth whispering to me. Gentle. Breathy. This was what it must be like, then, to sit in a dark car with her head resting on my shoulder. This was what it must be like for her to lean towards me in a dark movie theater and whisper something in my ear, what it must be like to feel her wrap her arms around me on a hammock under a blue summer sky, sighing with contentment.

And then Anthony Hasbourd's voice trumpeted in, brazen and obnoxious. He was strident in a discordant way; his showmanship was full of pretentious pomp and circumstance. They clapped for him anyway, long and hard. Midway through the song, he took Naomi's hand. I saw her flinch in surprise, then blush. They sang like that, hand in hand. At the end of the song, they embraced.

And that was what did me in. I cut my eyes away. And just like that, it was decided. No matter what it took, I would get the lead role at school. It didn't make a difference that I was just the understudy. I would land it somehow. Because I had something. Something that would stun Naomi. Astound her. I could sing. Sing lights-out brilliant. I would show the school. I'd show the world. I'd show all the pretenders out there. Most of all, I'd show Naomi.

★

VOICE LESSONS

For the next few months, before my mother awoke, I biked to school in the near dark. Cold and twilight darkness were my constant companions. The roads were always desolate and bitingly frigid; it always took me at least twenty minutes to thaw myself once at school. I would stand in the restroom and run my hands under the hot tap water, legs pressed hard against the radiator until I felt the heat begin to singe through my jeans. Then I'd walk into the music room warmed and ready. Mr. Matthewman would glance at me and fold his newspaper away. He never knew I biked to school. He would not have allowed it, given the Justin Dorsey incident.

We would go through scales at first, loosening up the— in his words—windpipes of melody. My voice box would be stiff and cramped at first, but he started me easy. C major scale over and over until I felt my voice box melting and moistening into readiness. Every so often he would stop and push his hand hard against my back. "Posture," he would say. "Gotta have good posture, Kris. Align that spine, and you'll be able to lift your chest easy, get a full breath of air in there. Remember the marionette."

The marionette was his illustration, something he'd taught to hundreds of students while at Julliard. The idea was to imagine two strings holding me up like a marionette, one attached to the top of my head and the other to my sternum. I was to maintain a posture that would keep the strings taut, especially on the exhale. It took a while to get used to.

He tutored me for about thirty minutes in the beginning. "Easy does it," he'd say. "Don't need to push you too hard for now." The time always flew by. I would look up from the notes, my eyes rising above the plane of the piano for the first time, and be astonished to see the parking lot outside filling up. Over time, I started staying longer, another fifteen, twenty minutes, until I found myself staying for a whole hour.

"I'll make you a singer yet," he would say enthusiastically. "I guarantee you. You watch."

No matter how late it was, we ended the lessons in the same way. He would sigh, glance my way, and say, "You know you're not going to get the role, Kris. It's beyond my power. The decision's not mine to make." I would nod at that, but I wonder if he ever sensed the quickening beat of my heart, the thinning of my lips. For I had my own plan. I would become so spectacular, prove myself to be such a prodigy, that my singing would expose Anthony Hasbourd for the charlatan he was. Then they would simply *have* to replace him with me. Then they would want to. The thought made me giddy, drunk with excitement: that I would one day supplant him by "popular demand." Popular. Demand. These two words were alien and foreign and had never applied to me, but they were words that thrilled me, nonetheless, to death.

OCTOBER 22

Winston Barnes was the next student murdered. I didn't really know him even though he'd sat next to me for weeks now. He was a shy boy, kept mostly to himself. During class he usually sat hunched over his desk, rarely looking up from his books. But he was always listening, his skinny elbows jutting outwards like white ears. He still let his mom cut his hair, and it showed. But he was a smart kid. Some said that come graduation in three years, he'd be giving Naomi a run for her money for class valedictorian. I didn't think so. She was Harvard quality, and he was merely a Cornell or Columbia. They got along well enough with each other, and I'd catch them in conversation every so often, discussing homework and whatnot. When he was with Naomi, he was like a different person. Positively chatty, as a matter of fact. Once, he bumped into us in the food court at the mall. I had to go somewhere, but when I returned half an hour later, he was still there talking to Naomi. Jeez.

I saw arrogance in him once, though. He was ribbing the new girl, Jan Blair, about a D- she'd received on a test, waving his A+ in her face. It seemed so out of character. Other than that, he was the kind of guy whose niceness made you want to throw up in your mouth a little.

Which was why his behavior that Wednesday afternoon was so inexplicable.

It was during yet another interminable, mind-numbingly boring class with Miss Winters, and half the class was drifting to sleep.

I was the first to notice. It started with my desk vibrating, humming ever so slightly. I glanced over at Winston; he was bobbing his leg up and down in agitation.

I grabbed the corners of my desk, steadying it, and turned to look at Winston again. His kneecap jerked against the desk harder, faster; an eraser fell off his desk, jostled by the constant shaking. He turned his head towards the window, but it was a slow, laborious act as if a giant elastic band restricted his movement. Something outside must have caught his attention; even from behind, I could see his body stiffen suddenly. I craned my neck past him and scanned the scenery outside. There was nothing but the wide-open spaces of the snow-laden baseball diamond. A few branches swayed ever so slightly. The sun shone unabashedly. The school flag lay limp against the pole, lifeless.

He began to tremble now, his arms gripping the top of his desk as if he were capsizing. The whites of his knuckles blended with the glare of snow outside. A whimper escaped his mouth.

The room seemed to turn prickly with anticipation, as if an electric charge were building. The colors of the room drained to gray; the contours of the furniture around me tightened. It was as if—

"Miss Winters!" shouted Winston. His voice exploded out like a cannon, startling the class. "Miss Winters!"

"Winston?" Miss Winters asked, jolted pale. She glanced outside the window. "What is it?"

"Miss Winters! Miss Winters!"

"What? Whatever is the matter, Winston?" There was genuine panic in her voice; her right hand dabbed her O-shaped mouth as with a napkin.

He stood up at that, gesturing wildly with his spindly arms, pointing outside. He was deathly pale now and sweating profusely. "Lock the door. Oh, please lock the door, Miss Winters!"

"Why?" She took a nervous step towards him. "What's the matter?"

For a few seconds, he said nothing. He sank down into his chair as if it were all over, taking a few furtive looks outside. Students were now half sitting, half standing in their chairs.

"Winston, tell me what's the matter!"

What I remember most about the next moment was the surreal aura. Miss Winters making her way towards Winston, nervous step by nervous step. Winston shaking as if the temperature had just plummeted twenty degrees. Motes of dust floating in midair, specks caught in the beams of sunlight. Miss Winters walking through those beams like a blue whale about to surface. Winston pointing outdoors with his skinny index finger, the beak of a chicken pecking away. The clock ticking ever so slowly. Winston's arm unintentionally sideswiping a book off the table. The heavy thud as it hit the floor. Miss Winters beseeching Winston again to tell her what was wrong, what was the matter. Winston pointing with exaggerated force at the empty fields outside. And, finally, opening his mouth to speak.

"Tell him to stop staring at me!"

And his pointing, gesturing, out towards the desolate fields, pointing, pointing to barren grounds of emptiness.

"Tell him to stop following me!"

"Who, Winston? Who are you talking about?" she sputtered in growing fear, spittle dotting her chin.

"The boy! Tell him to stop! Go out and tell him to stop!"

"I don't know...I don't see any—"

"The boy!"

I looked outside again. No one.

"The boy!" His voice was getting louder.

Miss Winters looked outside, then back at Winston, then back outside, her double chin swaying pendulum-like.

"The boy! With the red jacket! The red jacket!"

"Winston!"

"The red jacket! The red jacket!"

Miss Winters moved in on him then, her own fear suddenly rearing up on her. Her hefty fingers wrapped themselves tightly around his skinny arm. Not until she reached the principal's office did she release him.

There was a stunned silence when the classroom door slammed behind them. I kept waiting for a snide comment, for someone to call Winston a wuss or a weirdo. For someone to start laughing or to crack a joke. But no one said a thing.

Outside, a single bird etched its lonely flight across the sky. Otherwise it was absolutely still. Across the fields, beyond the far fence, stood the forest, dark and dormant. A few clouds drifted feebly as if unsure of where to go next. Then more clouds arrived. These were darker, denser, filled with determination. And the classroom darkened ever so slightly, as if it were a boat sinking away from the surface of the ocean and into its depths.

My fingers were shaking. I took a look around the classroom. Strange. Jan Blair was sitting taut in her seat, face turned down, ashen and pale. Like she was guilty of something. As if she had a dirty little secret. Her hands cupped her elbows. She was shaking slightly, her lower lip trembling, caving in on itself. And her fingers looked snapped, like the broken neck of a white swan. I turned to look outside again.

Miniscule flakes of snow were drifting downwards. There was no one out there.

The clouds gathered over the next hour. A state emergency weather notice was sent to all local schools warning of a powerful snowstorm front that had suddenly turned southeast. At 1:56 p.m., all schools were ordered closed for the day. A terrific yell echoed around the school when the announcement was made over the PA system. Teachers cautioned students to return home immediately and not linger. Their warnings were unnecessary; there was a near stampede as students slammed lockers and ran out of school.

I stood around Naomi's locker trying to appear as if I wasn't waiting for anyone in particular. But the minutes passed, and the flow of students thinned. There was no sign of her anywhere.

With the library closed, the only other place I could think she might be was the restroom. The corridor was empty now, and I could feel my feet gathering speed under me. In the quiet I could hear my boots squeaking a little. Outside the girls' bathroom I hesitated, then I opened the door a crack. "Naomi?" Not a sound in return. "Naomi!" I said, this time louder. My own echo came back at me, jolting me.

I'd never been in a girls' restroom before; it was a lot more spacious than the boys'. Facing the north side, there was a large window, something the boys' restroom lacked. It was snowing more heavily now, sheets of snow plummeting down in panicky droves. It startled me to see how desolate it had become outside. All the school buses, gone. Almost every car, gone. Only one lone figure walking across the fields, bent over against the gusting snow.

But there were footsteps outside, getting louder. The crisp sound of heels hitting the marbled floor. A woman's brisk steps. Clutching my book bag tight against my shoulder, I ducked into the nearest stall, closing the door behind me. I put the seat down and stood up on it, wobbling slightly. The restroom door swung opened.

The clicking sound of heels approached me, then stopped. Silence. *Click, click.* Then the sound of water running, hands being washed. The faucet turned off; more silence. I closed my eyes, the tension almost unbearable.

A cell phone rang.

"Hello?" It was the voice of Ms. Oliverson, a ninth grade history teacher. She spoke in loud, jarring tones, and her words echoed off the tiled walls.

"Yes...yes. Uh-huh. Should be home in about an hour. Uh-huh." I could hear her shoes tapping impatiently. "Uh-huh. Need to finish up a few things first. Uh-huh." She suddenly breathed in loudly, impatiently. "Look," she said, "I understand that the kids need to be picked up, but I have things I need to finish up here." Her voice was edgy, strained. "Something happened here today with a kid, you know, and—" She stopped suddenly, and for a span of five, six seconds, there was silence. "It's pretty serious," she continued, her voice calmer but shaky. "We think it's a bullying case. Uh-huh. No, no, someone from outside, an out-of-towner, we think. Don't know. He was saying something about a short man or a kid following him home last night, watching him through his bedroom window all night, stalking him to school this morning. Uh-huh. Really weird stuff. No. He wasn't really coherent; we don't know what to think. No, he's a good kid, really. Uh-huh. Look, I need to go…Can you?" She sniffed once, twice. "Bye."

Ms. Oliverson didn't leave the bathroom after that. She walked to the window directly in front of the stall I was in. From where I stood I could see the top of her head just clearing the top of the door. I crouched down a little more, carefully. There was a pert metallic click, the sound of a flare, then the trails of smoke meandering up towards the ceiling. I felt a tingling along the insides of my nostrils. A sneeze coming on. I stayed in that half-crouched position until my legs began to throb in pain. I tensed them, willing them to stop vibrating; any sound would have been magnified tenfold in that stall. She turned suddenly, her heels rapping concisely against the marble-tiled floor. She was right outside, facing the door of the stall, her arm probably reaching out to push it open. I closed my eyes and hunkered down lower, the words, *I'm sorry, Ms. Oliverson*, forming on my tongue.

Except she never came in. The click-clock of her heels moved past the stall and out the restroom. It was quiet again after that. I lowered myself and sat down. My back was slick with a cold dampness.

Winston Barnes was escorted home by his blustery mother. He'd been initially inconsolable in the principal's office, and he refused to speak. Even back at home, all he wanted to do was go to his room and sleep. With the lights on. In the morning, after having slept for fourteen hours, he got up fresh and rejuvenated. He was nothing if not bright and cheerful. He was even willing to laugh off the previous day's episode. His mother gave him an extra slice of bacon. She was glad he was back to normal; now that she thought about it, he had seemed tired and lackluster of late. Nothing that a good night's sleep couldn't fix. Winston Barnes picked up his school backpack, his lunch bag, and his gym shoes, kissed his mother on the cheek, and walked out the door into the semidarkness of early dawn. He was never seen alive again.

THE NEW YORK TIMES

OCTOBER 24

Over the last few weeks, the community of Ashland, New York, has been recovering from the harrowing murder of 16-year-old Justin Dorsey. And now another child has disappeared under equally disturbing circumstances. The latest disappearance of Winston Barnes, 15 years old, has confirmed what many have suspected and feared. A serial child killer is on the loose. "We have a serial kidnapper roaming our streets," said Ashland Police Chief Adam Geller yesterday at a terse press conference. "Watch your children, be on your guard, be vigilant."

Citizens of Ashland are trying their hardest in this difficult time. Hundreds volunteered to comb the wooded area behind Barnes's residence, but most were openly skeptical of finding anything helpful. "There's snow lying everywhere. If he went into the woods, we'd have seen the tracks already. Smooth as a baby's cheek," said Marsha Quinn, a neighbor.

"Nobody's coming out anymore," said Nathaniel Jones, a deli storeowner on Main Street.

"Kids are going straight back home after school; parents are shuttling them to and fro. Everybody's staying home, watching the kids, watching TV."

The principal of Slackenkill High School, Mr. Jonathan Marsworth, has come under considerable pressure to close the school down for a few days. He has so far refused to relent. A schoolteacher speaking on condition of anonymity said that most parents actually preferred having their children come to school, believing that being among friends would help to restore a sense of normalcy. All after-school activities have been canceled, excepting rehearsals for the school musical. Mr. Marsworth has continued to emphasize the communal importance of that show.

NOVEMBER 3

Fear descended on Ashland like black snow. An undertow of leftover angst from Justin Dorsey's disappearance reared itself. Gossip in the supermarkets and hair salons tightened, voices hushed with strain. Reporters from nearby counties arrived and started to probe around. A heightened police presence patrolled the streets, and Slackenkill High School hired three more security officers to walk the grounds. The county sheriff gave a talk on safety at a school assembly.

Naomi, bubbly and aghast at the same time, was all over the story. Every day, she spun out new theories on what had happened, mostly based on what she'd been reading online. "I'm telling you," she said, "the killer's gotta be someone we all know. A teacher. Another student."

I looked incredulously at her. "Don't be ridiculous. And maybe you haven't noticed, but people are dying. Students you know. Maybe you shouldn't be so cavalier about this whole thing."

"It could be true."

"Now you're just being ridiculous."

We were walking home after school, a now common day when neither of us had any after-school commitments. The snow on the ground was fluffy, breaking away like sand when we kicked at it. Traffic was light on the cleared roads. Still, I was glad that I'd left my bike at home today, for this time with Naomi.

"But it is so baffling," she continued. "Just *puff*, disappeared."

"I thought the police found some unusual tire markings near where Winston lived," I said. "Somebody came and picked him up. Or kidnapped him. Or lopped off his head and carried him in, piece by piece, if you want. But it's probably that simple: he was whisked away, willingly or not, by a car. That's where the police should be focusing their attention. On those tire marks, on a car."

"Oh, that is so five minutes ago, Xing. Of course they've already done that. And the fact that they haven't fed the media a description of a car just goes to show that there's nothing there. It's been too quiet. No word on anything. I think they're totally perplexed over the whole thing. Personally," she said breezily, "I think they need to be focusing on the students. It's one of us. There're enough oddballs and nut jobs walking around school."

"You should speak," I said.

"Oh, shut up," she replied tersely. "You're my number one suspect, truth be told. Or should be. Quiet, withdrawn, inscrutable. In fact, if I didn't know you any better, I'd really think you were a ticking time bomb, like that Seung-Hui Cho psycho. You know, the Virginia Tech guy."

Her words stung. Quickly, I said, "Yeah, right, you have no—"

"Why are you like that, Xing?" she asked, suddenly serious. There was a long, torturous pause. I could feel her eyes turning to me. "Why can't you just be normal with everyone the way you are with me? Why do you clam up at school so much?"

"That's not true; I get along fine with everyone."

"You so do not. Honestly, sometimes even I look at you and think you're a freakball. And the thing that gets me is you're not. But you skulk around school barely saying anything; some people don't even think you speak English. They think you got off the boat yesterday. You don't know how many times I've heard people making fun of you behind your back, saying you're stockpiling guns at home. You should hear the stuff that's said."

"Haha dee ha ha, you're a bucket of laughs today. What gives you the right to take the social high ground on me? It's not like you're swarmed by friends at school, is it? Who made you Miss Congeniality?"

"Yeah, right," she spat out, and her words hung between us.

For a few minutes we did not speak. The sun fell behind the woods, and the air noticeably chilled. Faint etches of color still painted the sky, but they were fading. Our steps, once hurried in anger, gradually slowed.

Naomi took an apple out of her backpack. "Didn't have time to get to this over lunch." She took a few more bites, then handed me the furrowed remainder. Little spittles of saliva dotted the edge of her bite marks. I devoured the apple, savoring every bite, and threw the rutted core into the woods on our right.

"Litterbug," she said softly. She didn't say more, but it was enough. She glanced at me briefly; her brown eyes were startling against the snowy background.

"You should zip up your jacket," I said. "Getting cold."

"Can't," she said. "It's jammed."

"Here. Let me." And she did, to my surprise. I whipped off my gloves and placed my hands on her jacket. She looked down at my hands, chapped coarse at the knuckles. The zipper was ensconced with snow, and I had to brush at it, softly. I pulled hard, and the zipper came free.

"You need hand cream," she said softly.

I nodded in agreement; we started to walk again, this time slower.

"You need a new jacket," I said. She smiled sadly. We both knew that there would be no hand cream for me, and no new jacket for her. Neither of us had the money.

When Naomi first appeared at my elementary school years ago, it was already halfway through the academic year. A total FOB, not a lick of English, her hair still done up in Chinese ponytails, for crying out loud. She had worn a pink winter jacket, a bright puffy jacket in which she took obvious delight. She loved the shine of it, the little bunny embroidered across the pocket. At first recess, a circle of students had surrounded her. She didn't understand a word they said, but they were smiling and laughing. She smiled back, as warmly as she could, glad to be accepted. But then she saw that the smiles were nothing more than jeers, and the laughter was nothing but the sound of derision. They weren't asking her to play—they were yelling *"Playboy"* at her, pointing, then jabbing their fingers into the rabbit emblem on her jacket.

Then they began to pelt her with snowballs. Her jacket deflected most of the powdery snowballs. It did nothing, however, for the rock thrown viciously at her head. It cut her open, an ugly gash just under her left eye.

A teacher had come to her rescue and taken her inside to the medical room. The nurse tried to reassure her, but Naomi did not understand a word. That was when they called me in.

As soon as I stepped into the room, recognition came into her eyes even though we'd never met before. After they pushed me towards her, she whispered to me in Cantonese, gladness welling in her eyes. The things I still remember: her hair dotted with the glistening beads of melted snow, a single tear escaping her eyes, quickly wiped away with the back of her hand. They could not stanch the blood; it kept seeping through the bandages. Naomi lay on her back, eyes clenched shut against the pain. And before I knew it, the nurse grabbed Naomi's hand and placed it in mine. Naomi held my hand tightly. Her skin was silky smooth, and for some reason that surprised me. I tried to squirm my hand away, but she only tightened her grip. She never let go.

After I dropped Naomi off at the bus stop, I headed home. As if on cue, the weather instantly turned sour. Gusts of wind tore down the street, sharp as scalpels. I pulled my winter hat down and shriveled into the recesses of my jacket. Frail branches trembled in the wind like the last spasms of death. Dusk faded with cold resignation into night, and the spreading darkness enveloped me with disquieting speed.

Quickening my pace, I passed a murky enclave of trees. It was widely rumored that Jan Blair—the freakish new girl— had moved somewhere inside there with her father, a feral, bearded man who took long hunting trips. I hurried over a short bridge, the water under it already frozen.

The wind whistled again, sharpening against itself. I had a decision to make. I could continue on this road, a circuitous but relatively easy way home. Or I could cut across the woods on my right, cutting short my walk by ten minutes. Right then, a gust of wind howled and sliced through my face. To the woods I went.

But not a minute later, I realized I'd made a mistake. Night was at least an hour more advanced in the dense woods. Before too long, I was forced to walk with outstretched arms, mummy-like in the solidifying darkness.

There are realizations which arrive as suddenly as a submarine breaking surface. Then there are those that arrive much slower, as with the rising of the morning sun. And that's how I realized I was being followed: gradually, by osmosis, if you will. There was no sudden snapping of a twig or the crunch of snow. Just a dawning sense until, somehow, I knew.

Somebody's eyes were focused on me, watching my every move. I stopped and listened.

In the abyss of blackness that cloaked the trees, someone was there. Standing just outside the periphery. Watching me.

And so, I thought to myself, this was where Trey Logan would exact his revenge. He'd taken his time, but Naomi was right. He hadn't forgotten. I'd seen him around school sporadically over the last few weeks, the black eye slowly turning to green, then gray until it finally faded away altogether. I should have known he'd wait until the bruising went away. All the better for him to gloat with pink skin while I went around in contrasting black and blue. I should have known.

"Why don't you come out where I can see you, Logan?" I said it in a whisper. In such stillness, he could have heard a butterfly sighing.

Silence.

"I know you're back there. Come out where I can see you."

Again, no response.

I squinted deeper into the darkness. Did I see a shifting in the darkness, a twirling in the current of shadows? He stayed in there, biding his time.

A mammoth fear—something even Logan was incapable of causing—tumbled into my consciousness. Logan was not this sophisticated in his approach. He was all broad strokes, no subtlety or nuance. He knew nothing of the art of ambush.

There was something else in the woods with me.

Darkness breathed with me, heavier.

I turned and ran.

And as I did, I heard the unabashed sounds of branches snapping, the rustling of clothes behind me. Of somebody giving chase.

I forgot time; I forgot exhaustion. A kaleidoscope of spinning darkness whirled around and past me. Singeing hot air rushed up my windpipes, and stinging cold air gushed down in swift tandem.

He was fast, stubborn, never veering far from me, always directly in line behind me. Try as I might, I could not lose him, not even in the black obscurity. I ran as if by instinct through puddles of darkness. My skin prickled with the anticipation of being touched by cold, chicken-skin hands, thin fingers eager to grasp my exposed neck. Only once did I glance backwards and saw a hazy shadow like an inkblot moving towards me. I made out a dash of red, a red jacket.

And then I was through. Openness burst before me: the rush of airy gray, the wide gossamer sky above, the nakedness of the barren road. I tumbled down a short bank to the road, my legs trying to catch up under me.

Something tripped me—a sudden dip in the bank, perhaps—and flattened me on the ground. My breath *humphed* out. I lay shattered in the snow like a rock embedded in the cracked web of a windscreen, waiting for him.

Was this how Justin Dorsey felt in his last moments? Was this how Winston Barnes felt in the disquieting moments when death became inevitable? For me, there were no flashbacks of my life set in slow motion to the cadence of soft music. Only the throbbing expectation of horrific pain, and a small, sick curiosity as to how it would be done. With a switchblade, an axe, a gun? Would he do me in right there or secrete me to somewhere private? I felt a curiosity about the killer, too. A hulking lunatic, blood smeared on face? Or a quiet Lilliputian face, shy and pleasant, even?

But he never came. My breath steadied until it was quiet again. Haltingly I stood up, trying to ground my unsteady legs beneath me. The road stretched out before me, isolated, not a dot of light to be found. And the woods, though looming in darkness, were oddly benign, as if they could not be blamed for any danger contained within.

I walked up the slight bank, backtracking. I found my own tracks in the snow, messy gashes, panic written all over them.

I did not find his prints on the bank. He had stayed in the forest and refused to emerge. I stared into the woods, sensing eyes observing me. Backpedaling, I began to move away quickly, carefully to the road. My eyes never left the woods.

Nothing moved in that darkness; nothing made a sound.

CHINATOWN

Nothing moved in the darkness; nothing made a sound. That morning when I woke up, all was still at first. Then I sensed my father standing beside me, his hand gently tugging my shoulder.

"Xing. It's time to go."

We arrived in Chinatown early on that summer morning. A few stragglers walked the gray streets, sunshine glinting against the dirt gravel. Sullen buildings surrounded us like ashen tombstones. In Grand Street Park, a battalion of grandmothers, swathed in their traditional Chinese garb, moved in slow motion, arms extended, the gentle span of their bent arms swirling to cut through the fusty air. In a few hours their gentle lullaby of motion would be replaced by the rapid rancor of street basketball; but for now a sedate quality prevailed.

My father and I hunkered down at a rickety table in a little hole in the wall. We slurped at our bowls filled to the brim with speckled thousand-year egg congee. Occasionally, we sipped our tea, gazing outside at the grandmothers at their tai chi. Then on cue, as if by an internal alarm clock, my father looked across the table at me and asked with a look, "Well?"

We made our way over to the corner of Mott and Canal. It was a little early for most tourists, but not too early to stake our land. Later on in the day, every street corner would be taken over by street vendors hawking their goods: sellers of counterfeit DVDs, bootleg copies of the most recent Top 10 albums, five-dollar I Love New York T-shirts, calligraphers, masseuses astride their makeshift benches.

For the first two hours, my father dillydallied. It was, as usual, the best part of the day, the part when my father taught me his craft. Back in China, he'd been quite the prodigy at his art school. And it was in these lull times when I saw the artisan, when my father wrapped his hand over mine, held the brush, and, giving instruction in deep monotones, maneuvered my hand. I loved seeing the images form, the sensation of my father's spirit flowing through my own and spilling out onto the canvas. The pandas we produced, the tigers, the butterflies, the bamboo, the floating water lilies.

Around noon, the trickle of tourists gorged into a flood. I sat next to my father, sometimes chatting with the customers, but mostly I just watched him work. The tourists always walked by gawking, but the local Chinese passed by with indifference.

And then, a horrible nightmare.

In the middle of the crowd, standing in front of my father, was Gina Summers with her family.

I froze.

Gina Summers was a classmate, one of the nicest girls I knew. With her blue eyes, blonde hair, and sparkling personality, she was the epitome of all-American beauty. She was one of the few students who didn't talk slowly or use simple words when speaking to me.

The truth was that I was deeply ashamed of what my father did. I felt myself cringing inwardly, anticipating that awful moment when Gina Summers would spot me. I went to a school where students were well bred, immaculately groomed, suave, and hip, whose parents were CEOs and doctors and partners of law firms. Not Chinatown hawkers. Not Charlie Chan kowtow specialists who spoke in choppy, sloppy Chinglish, who took in with grubby hands crumpled dollar bills, who were told to keep the change and invariably did.

I did not want her to know. That the man in front of her was my father. That I was the son of this rust-toned, sunken-cheeked vendor.

I put my head down into my hands and turned around. The minutes passed interminably.

"Almost finish, OK. I add some red, then finish, OK?" my father finally said to Gina.

"What did he say?" someone from her group asked.

"I paint red, I finish real nice," my father said, louder.

In the protracted silence that followed, I sensed the giggles being stifled behind me, the amused glances being shared.

"*Ah, Xing,*" my father suddenly said to me, "*bei ngoh baat mun.*" He needed change.

To hand over the money to my father was to blow my cover. I would have to turn and uncover my face, and Gina Summers would surely see me.

So I flaked, something I would never forgive myself for. I just got up and left.

At first, I walked quickly, but I slowed down after a few minutes. I sat down on the benches at Grand Street Park. Basketball hoodlums were out in full force. The elderly ambled around the park. The sun began to dip, and when it finally disappeared behind a gray building hours later, I trudged slowly back to the street corner.

My father was already packed up. He didn't say anything when I walked up to him. I thought he might be angry, might even scold me for deserting him. But when he picked up his case, he looked at me in a tender, understanding way. "Well? Are you about ready to go now?" he asked, softly.

We made our way through Chinatown slowly, meandering along the emptying streets. At a traffic light, my father put his arm around my shoulder, gentle yet firm. It was full of warmth. The light turned green; we began to walk.

"I went to the park," I said, my voice soft with guilt.

My father nodded.

"Just wanted to stretch my legs a bit."

My father looked at me, not with unkindness. "Don't worry," he said. "We did well today. Lots of customers. We can buy some fruit for Mom tonight."

We stopped in front of a fruit store. With nimble fingers, my father picked up oranges in turn, lightly squeezing each one before dropping them into a red plastic bag. Under the harsh store light, the wrinkles etched into my father's face seemed to deepen. There were untold stories of sorrow buried deep in them.

My father smiled to himself. "Your mother will like these oranges. We can surprise her when we get home," he said as he handed over the bills. There were light flecks of red paint on his fingers.

The stores were shutting down now, metal doors grating nosily downwards over entrances. Lights were switched off, and tired voices spoke with minimal words.

My father peeled an orange as we walked. "Here," he said, handing a piece to me.

It was bittersweet.

─────── ★ ───────

We took the Metro North home, a quiet journey back. I slept for most of it. Walking home from the train station, my father died. He was killed. A pickup truck, driven much too fast, careened around the corner and skidded. There was a sudden, vicious intrusion of noise and hulking metal. The skidding vehicle missed me by no more than two feet—can you feel the whip-breeze of a skidding car from more than two feet away?—but hit my father dead on. I heard—but did not see—a sickening, splatty thud, like a bottle of ketchup dropped and shattered.

The pickup truck sat at the edge of the road as if stunned; then it took off quietly down the road and disappeared around the corner.

I could not find my father. He had been knocked clear over some bushes and fifteen yards into the dark woods. How was I supposed to know? How was I to know a person could be propelled that far away? I looked into the woods, fearful. Nothing moved in the darkness; nothing made a sound.

I ran home, dizzy with nauseous waves of self-denial. I was full of fear and confusion, each feeding into the other. As the undeniable, awful truth seeped in, tears spilled out like acid out of a dropper. I ran up the driveway, my heart dislodging from my ribcage.

A late dinner was being cooked; I could hear the sizzle of meat frying on the stove.

"You're finally back!" my mother said from within the kitchen. The screen door slammed shut behind me. "I cooked your favorites tonight," she said in a breezy voice.

NOVEMBER 3, EVENING

I was breathless when I reached home, my legs past gone. Every few steps I'd glance back, convinced I'd see the red-jacketed man still chasing me down. I walked up the driveway, my clothes still caked with snow and dirt. A light was on in the kitchen. I was freezing and weary. I was going to crash soon.

My mother was sitting at the kitchen counter, a cup of tea in hand. She stood up as I entered and peered intently at me. "What happened, Xing? You look like you've seen a ghost." She used the Chinese word *gui* for ghost—a female apparition with long black hair covering her face who, having died due to misfortune, returns for revenge.

Yes, I wanted to say, *and the* gui *is standing right in front of me.* I took off my backpack and put it down at my feet. "You're home early tonight."

"Is everything OK?" she asked.

"Yeah."

"You don't look all right." She glanced at my clothes. "Did you fall down?"

"It's nothing."

"What happened?"

"Just, you know."

She placed her hands on her hips. "Tell me what happened."

"Nothing."

She bit her lower lip, frustrated. "This is not the time to be hiding stuff from me, Xing. Did something happen? With all the disappearances, you need to let me know if you see something strange."

I nodded. "I will." For a microsecond I met her gaze before I flicked my eyes away to the side. She had aged so much in recent years, sometimes it caught me by surprise. Wrinkles I had not seen, a new caution in her eyes, a sudden droop at the corners of her mouth. Somewhere along the way she had gone from being my mother to someone else's grandmother. "I was just having a snowball fight with Naomi. Kind of embarrassed about it; it was pretty childish what we did."

Her look softened instantly. "Oh, there's nothing childish about playing in the snow."

"I'm sorry. I'll try to be back before nightfall next time."

"I let you get away with far too much, Xing." She paused. "You're not supposed to be walking the streets alone; I thought we talked about this already."

"We did, we did. Today was just an exception."

"Naomi's parents still driving you home every night, right?"

"They are," I lied. "They've been really good about that."

"And you're taking the school bus in the morning, right?"

"Of course," I said, smiling. With her late hours, she never woke up before I left the house. "Who'd want to walk or bike in this weather, anyway? It's been crazy—can't believe it's snowed so much already."

That seemed to appease her. She picked up her teacup and made her way up the stairs.

"Don't forget to turn off the lights when you come up," she said from outside her bedroom. "Don't forget to do your homework—you make me worry. Dinner's in the kitchen." The door closed with a muffled finality. The television turned on.

On the kitchen counter was a saran-wrapped sandwich, peanut butter and jelly. I ignored it, moving to the stove where I turned on all the ranges. I watched the flames dance before me, a myriad of flickering blue and orange and purple and red. Slowly, the room filled with heat, but I needed more. Cold had settled deep into my bones.

I sat down at the kitchen table and, using my forearm as a pillow, leaned my head down. I was too tired to walk up to my room. I would sleep awhile here. And I knew that Miss Durgenhoff would come down shortly. I didn't know how I knew this. But she would be down very soon.

The sound of cutlery being laid on the table. The smell of chicken broth simmering. The clink of plates placed on the kitchen counter. The room a toasty warm. I opened my eyes.

Miss Durgenhoff was at the stove, her stooped back to me. Without turning, she said, "Ah, you're up now. Was just about to wake you." She brought me a bowl of soup.

It was, of course, just what I wanted. The broth sank luxuriously into my stomach, warming my insides.

"Perfect for this time of night," she said. "Not too heavy to bloat, but textured enough to fill. Mind you, it'll help you to sleep, too, not that you'll have difficulty with that tonight."

"What time is it?" I asked, my head slowly spinning.

"Oh, late enough, I suppose," she said. Night had fallen outside, turning the window into a perfect mirror. I caught my reflection. My body was slouched was over to the point I was almost facedown in the soup. My hair a frazzled mess. There were sleep lines on my cheek where the creases of my sleeves had grooved in.

I was drinking my last spoonful when she pushed the saran-wrapped sandwich towards me. "Eat this," she said. She saw my expression and urged me, "Come now, she at least made the effort. You should eat it."

I was too tired to argue. I pulled the sandwich toward me and partially unwrapped it. It looked like a dead rodent to me, cold to the touch and stiff. I poked at it. "Can you turn off the light, please? It's too bright."

In the semidarkness, the purple flames of the stove cast a flickering, pooled glow. It was very quiet; there was only a faint hissing from the stove. And it was black outside, the darkness draping over the windowpane like a thickened curtain, the mirrored reflection lost.

"Cold out. Windy, too," she murmured to herself.

My head drooped again, a load of sleep weighing it down. I thought I'd be too drowsy to talk, but the words seemed to slip easily off my tongue. My voice, cupped in the elbowed cave of my arm, was deep and mature. "I walked Naomi to the bus stop. We got into a little argument. No big deal. But it got late."

The chair creaked as she settled herself into a more comfortable position.

I paused, wondering if I should say more. "And then coming here, I just…"

"Yes?"

"I took a shortcut. Through the woods."

"And something in there spooked you?" she asked.

I paused. "How did you know?"

"You've got little scratch marks across your face. Just tiny ones. Something that branches would do if brushed against quickly. You were running," she said matter-of-factly.

I touched my face gingerly and traced the thin etches. "Nothing spooked me," I said.

"Really?" she asked. Her moist eyes were depositories of sympathy.

"My legs feel like jelly now." I stretched them out. "I'm sure they're going to ache tomorrow." She didn't press. She only sat quietly, hardly there to me, but I knew she took measurement of my every word. For whatever reason, she cared for me. Back of all her eccentricities, there was something in her that reached out to me. I shut my eyes tighter, seeking a deeper darkness to escape into

She went to the stove and spooned out more soup from the dutch oven. "More?" she asked, sitting back down.

I shook my head, too tired to even lift it. But I could hear her drinking the broth, a faint sipping sound and then the swallow down her throat.

"I remember in my youth when I would spend whole days out in winters much harsher than this," she said. "Used to out-play my brothers, even, strong and hardy boys but no match for me. Three, four hours later they were no good for the outdoors, would have to go whimpering home for some fire and hot cocoa. Me—" she chuckled to herself, "I was still good for another hour. Only had to come in when the day grew dark and couldn't see beyond my arms anymore. Mama yelling at me to come in and get something to eat."

"You hardly go out now, though," I heard myself saying. "Most of the time you stay in your room."

She said nothing.

"What do you do all day?" I did not mean to be harsh. It was only that I was tired and didn't want to use a great many words. "Don't you get bored at all?"

"I think a lot." Her voice, too, was soft, bereft of self-defense. "At my age, there's a library of memories to peruse. I think back to places I've been to, friendships I've shared. My husband, those years we spent together. I've had some happy years, and I like to reflect upon them."

"Don't you ever want to go out? See this town a little? Meet people?"

"After a while," she said, "you see that every place is essentially the same. You come of age, and suddenly all places resemble each other. And people, too, for the most part, are basically the same, but even more so than places. All cut from the same cloth of gray. There isn't much left out there that I haven't already encountered in some shape or form. Most of it unremarkable and mundane, some of it downright ugly." She sighed softly, unconsciously. "My best years have already been lived."

It was quiet again. I heard her gathering the bowls and utensils together. "I can't wait to see the world," I whispered.

She stopped what she was doing as if to encourage me to continue. She was always doing that, trying to get me to talk more. So much of her actions were calculated to enter into a conversation with me. But never overbearingly. She was always careful not to smother me.

I thought I understood her a little better now, understood how in the empty waiting of her daily life, my return and an occasion for conversation could enliven her so. It bothered me that her happiness should be so tethered to me. But she sat so patiently now, her eyes—somehow I knew this—fixed not on my lowered head but on the empty plates and bowls before her, waiting and hoping, waiting, waiting. I lifted my head. Her eyes were soft and tentative, barely certain enough to stay level with mine. I thought to smile kindly at her.

"I've been having problems with this one kid at school. A few weeks ago I got into a fight with him. Him and two of his buddies. As it turned out," I said, gloating a bit, "I got the better of the situation. Actually, he ended up with a black eye."

"I remember that night," she said. "Weren't you somewhat hurt, if I recall correctly?"

"Yeah, but I definitely got the better of him that day," I said with emphasis.

"And tonight?"

"I don't know. I think he might have followed me, stalked me in the woods. It sounded like someone was following me."

Her face tightened as she tried to suppress a mounting alarm. She looked at me with a new focus. "What's his name?"

"Logan. Trey Logan. Otherwise known as the Idiot."

"And where does he live?"

I stared at her. "Excuse me?"

She shrugged her shoulders dismissively.

"You ask a lot of strange questions," I said to her.

She stood up and came back to the table with more food. "You must be tired. Have more food." She placed some chicken on my plate. "It will help you relax."

"Why do you want to know where he lives?"

She *tsked tsked* me and took dishes to the sink.

I felt a numbed alarm rise up in me. But perhaps it was because I was so sleepy that I said nothing and only stared at her washing the dishes. And then: the dimness of the room, the soporific sound of splashing in the sink—sleep fell on me, firm and heavy. And then, hastened by the dimness of the room and the soporific sound of splashing in the sink, sleep fell on me, firm and heavy.

I was in that sleepy netherland when I heard Miss Durgenhoff take her seat.

"You should go to bed now," she said. Her voice sounded very far away.

I thought about my bed upstairs, the long journey up the stairs. I would collapse on my bed and awake in the morning sore and smelly. I would take a shower, dry myself off with my dank, smelly towel, and get ready for school. There would be books to open, chairs to sit in, classes to attend. I knew what was going to happen the next day just as if it had already happened; it seemed tedious to have to go through the pretenses of actually living through it to make it real. It was all the same routine, all carried in the confines of school, house, room, and this small town, all with the same dreary repetition. I yearned for something more.

"One day I will leave this town," I said in a voice so soft the words seemed to float up delicately like ashes.

"And where will you go?" she asked after a moment.

I wanted to tell her. That place I went to in my dreams, a place I'd never spoken of, not even to Naomi. Where rattan fishing boats floated in sedentary waters under crimson skies; where lush grass rippled in the breeze before undulating hills; where the pristine air was so clear and pure that merely breathing it in rid the body of disease. This land that I not only belonged to but which somehow belonged to me, a place whose contours embraced and contained me even more completely than my own skin.

But I was too tired to speak. Sleep had enfolded me.

"Where it's beautiful," I murmured. My eyes closed.

"Shhhh..."

Sleep was overtaking me now. "Where nobody hates me..."

"Hush now. Nobody hates you."

"Almost everyone does…"

"Sleep." And she began to hum, a light lullaby somehow both foreign and familiar to me. But I hardly heard it at all. Her fingers stroked my hair. I drifted away.

NOVEMBER 20

M iss Winters rapped the chalk against the black-board like a jackhammer. Waiting a few dramatic seconds, she took a deep breath then informed us that we had a "special project" that day. She waved her meaty hand as she spoke.

"I understand that many of us have been under a strain lately. I understand that we've lost our sense of normalcy. Things are no longer the same. We don't have the same sense of security as we go about our daily business. We don't 'hang out' very much anymore, do we? Perhaps we're not sleeping as well at night."

She went on and on, interminably.

About five minutes later, she finally said, "So what I'm trying to say is we should do something different today." She bit her lower lip, her eyes glistening with maudlin wetness. "Yes, we shall do something different. For Winston. For Justin. For getting our minds off this mess. So I propose that we put away our books and, well, draw our feelings today."

A few heads turned to look at one another. Draw?

"What I'd like you to do is to find yourself a quiet spot in school and draw your feelings out. I'm handing out blank pieces of paper on which I'd like you to, oh, I don't know, to put your feelings down."

"Draw what?" somebody asked from the back.

"Your feelings. Express your feelings on paper."

"You want me to write down how I'm feeling," said the same voice.

"No. Draw. Draw your feelings out."

There was a pause. "I don't understand."

"Draw. Draw your feelings out," she said emphatically.

Another pause. "Oh. Draw my feelings out."

"Yes," she said, a little excitedly now, "let your feelings feel by expressing them. Through a drawing. Through *you* drawing."

There was another pause. Somebody else spoke up. "I don't get it."

Welcome to the wonderful world of learning at Slackenkill High.

We were paired up as a precautionary measure—Miss Winters thought it would be safer for us to do that "in light of recent affairs"—and though I was hoping to be assigned with Naomi, I was paired up with, of all people, Jan Blair. We dispersed, each pair cradling pencils, erasers, and two sheets of paper.

Jan Blair and I milled around the hallways for a while, trying to find a good spot. Personally, I thought the library would be the ideal place. There were tables and chairs to position ourselves, and if I got bored I could always check out that day's paper. Plus, I had a suspicion that Naomi and her partner were heading there.

But Jan Blair had other ideas. This surprised me; I didn't think she possessed any ideas. Yet she led me away from the library and told me that she had another place in mind. A place where it would be nice to draw.

She led me towards the auditorium. I could hear the chatter of other students thinning out as they headed—no surprise here—to the cafeteria, where there would no doubt join other friends who were chowing down. Whatever "feelings" they drew would probably be accompanied by ketchup smears and greasy hot dog stains.

The auditorium was empty. At first I thought we were going to sit on the stage, but she led me towards the back of the stage. She started climbing up some scaffolding that was being used to add lighting fixtures for the musical.

"Hey! Where are you going?"

She shimmied her way up to the planked platform about twenty feet up. Reaching the top, she swung her legs around and pulled herself onto the platform. Her chest heaved up and down from the exertion of her climb. "C'mon up!" she said. "It's awesome up here."

"I'll stay here," I said, trying to make my voice authoritative. "Anyway, I don't think we should be up there."

I had never spoken with this girl before, but she was looking at me with a directness I found unnerving.

"Scaredy cat," she sneered.

"Excuse me?"

"I said, 'Scaredy cat.'" She paused, studying me. "What are you going to do? Just sit there?" she asked.

"No. I've got my feelings to draw." I grimaced at the words.

"Well, good luck. 'Cause guess who's got all the paper and pencils."

She was right. "Oh, come on!" I protested.

"What d'ja say? You talk funny."

"C'mon! Throw them down."

"Come up and get 'em!"

I paused, then began to climb up the scaffolding. The rungs were unsteady.

"Careful," she said when I swung my feet onto the platform, "it's kind of wobbly and unstable. Walk here slowly."

I warily edged my way up. The platform was nothing more than a few planks of wood placed together. It felt woefully thin under me. I knelt down, breathing hard.

"I like climbing," she said gazing out to the empty rows of seats before us. "I climb all the time. Don't think there's a single tree in my woods I haven't climbed."

"I'm not sure I like it up here. We should go back down."

But she was looking at me with an idea in her eyes. "Wait. Gonna show you something real neat."

She stood up quickly and traversed her way down the plank. I felt it bounce and jostle under me.

"Where are you going? Just sit down."

She leaned over a rail, precariously, stretching her body taut as an anchor rope; her fingers at the end of her outstretched arm wriggled towards a light switch on the far wall. She came up short by about a foot or so, and I assumed she was going to give up.

But instead, she tiptoed and perched forward even more. Her skinny body went past the point of equilibrium, and she pitched forward, the whole force of momentum behind her now. My breath caught. But as her body toppled forward and almost over the rail, her fingers landed on the switch, turned it off, and pushed off against it. Her body nudged back past the railing. The whole auditorium plunged into semidarkness.

"I found that switch the other day when I was here," she said, sitting down next to me again, closer this time. "I love it when it's dark like this. Makes me feel like I'm a performer. All I can see are the first three rows, and everything else is just black. I can pretend it's a packed house, and out there are all my adoring fans. Like I'm performing at my very own concert." She flung up an arm in dramatic fashion and shimmied her lanky body.

Only the dim lights from above the stage were on now, lights frosted over with blue paint. They washed everything in a surreal glow. The lighting actually accommodated her, smoothing out a rash of acne and adding texture to her pasty skin. It brought shadows over her mouth, too, important for a girl whose smile exposed a crowded row of teeth all at Xs and Ys with each other.

I didn't really know anything about Jan Blair. Since her disastrous first-day introduction to the class, she'd proven herself to be as bland as the sound of her name. She hardly spoke and mostly kept to herself. There were some ugly rumors about her.

"I hear you got the backup thingie in the musical," she said to me. She was shy about it, not looking at me. She played with the chewed laces of her boots.

"Listen, let's go back down. What if someone comes in?"

"So?"

"Well, they might see us and think…" I didn't go on. "Just give me the paper."

She handed it over. In the dead center was her shoe print. "Don't complain," she said. "The other sheet is even worse. It's ripped almost in half. But I'll use it." She started chewing on her pencil, humming something unrecognizable.

Wait till I tell Naomi about this, I thought to myself. That'd get a laugh out of her.

Perched up on the scaffolding offered me a bird's-eye view of the stage. It was my first time seeing it. And the half-built stables, the mural of shepherds, and the metallic-wire frame of the Bethlehem star all made the show suddenly so real to me. Its magnitude. Its imminence.

"So is it true?" she asked. She wore an open look on her face.

"What is?" I murmured. Anytime now, somebody would walk in, turn on the lights, and catch us two sitting together. I could see it now: an endless stream of jokes about the two of us frolicking in the dark.

"The whole deal with you being the backup in the musical. Is it true?"

"I guess so." I worked my pencil up and down, etches of lines above an oval shape. A head, I realized.

"Hey, maybe Hasbourd will disappear just like the others. Then you'll have the lead."

"You shouldn't talk that way."

"OK, Dad."

I ignored her.

"Hey, why don't you sing now?" she suddenly suggested, her voice spry. She smiled, exposing her ramshackle teeth. "Let me hear you."

I decided the best approach was to ignore her. I concentrated on my drawing, thickening the lines, making the strokes thicker, more feral.

She persisted. "Can I come to watch you practice sometime?"

I didn't respond.

"Isn't there some song you could do right now?" She slapped me on the arm. "Oh, c'mon!"

"Look, why don't we not talk," I said, drawing a few more strokes.

She was quiet for a short time. "You know, I heard about your dad dyin' and all."

My pencil paused momentarily.

"I was askin' some girls in the locker room after gym class about you—"

"Who did you talk to?"

"Just some girls. They said your dad died in a real bad accident. Hit and run and all that s—"

"Listen, I don't want to talk about it."

"How long ago was it? Huh? How long ago?" she pestered.

"About five years," I said, hoping an answer would shut her up.

She counted off on her hands some crude math. "You must have been like in fourth or fifth grade."

"I suppose."

"Well, at least you were kind of young. Easier to get over." She paused, hesitating. "Right?"

"Listen, I don't know you. Why don't we just draw?"

"My ma's dead, too," she said quietly. Then, haltingly, she said, "It was a suicide."

I looked at her. She was wearing tight-fitting, faded jeans and a flimsy blouse with rakish spaghetti straps. Whitish lines of flecked skin were etched along her arms. "Let's just draw, OK?" I said.

"My father. He looks after me now. Just me and him and no one else in the whole world." She looked at me as if for a response.

I got back to my drawing.

"What cha drawing?"

"Nothing. Don't you think you should draw a little bit yourself?"

"Looks like it's something."

"Nothing."

"Well, sure now, it is something." She swiveled around to get a better angle, brushing up against me. "Looks like a boy or something."

I was momentarily taken aback. I'd been drawing no more than a head; but now, looking down, there had seemingly surfaced a whole portrait of a short, hulking figure. Running through the woods, a crescent moon hung above, wearing a jacket. A child's amateurish delineation, crude circles, distorted and disproportionate. I blinked.

Jan Blair was studying the drawing with a concentration I didn't think she was capable of. "Looks like..." she said before her voice drifted off. She turned to me and moved closer suddenly. I could smell a foul puff of rotten-egg breath wafting past my nose. "The jacket. I'd draw the same if I could. Make it red."

"Well, why don't you?" I said, not looking at her.

"Ain't got no artist in me."

"Well, just try," I answered, irritated. "Nothing to be lost in just trying. A person can do a lot simply by trying." I stared at the pencil; its lead end was whittled down into a smooth nub.

"You a preacher or something? Getting philosophysics... philosp...gettin' all religious on me now, are you?" She looked down at my drawing again. "What's with this person running in the woods?" she asked.

"I don't know," I answered.

"Then why did you draw him?"

"No reason. Just, you know. Just because."

"Cause what?"

"Nothing, really," I said.

"C'mon. Tell me." Her eyes sharpened into a sudden fierceness, keen and frantic. "Tell me, tell me, tell me," she said, tugging at my sleeve.

"It's nothing. Quit bugging me—"

"Why won't you just tell me?"

"Tell you what? I have no idea what you're going on about—"

"I saw you that day," she said. She hooked her body perpendicular to mine; a blue light hovering just behind her blurred the lineament of her face. "I saw you, Kris. That day when Winston Barnes went nuts in the classroom. I saw the way you looked. Like spooked out of your mind."

"What are you talking about?" I asked, even though I knew exactly what she was referring to. My heart was suddenly racing, cawing in my ribcage like a bird.

"The day when Winston shouted about the boy. *The red jacket! The red jacket!* He went off on that. I saw the way you looked, man—you were freaked out. I saw. I know. Don't deny it. You were worried about something."

I remembered—of course I did. And I also remembered the way she looked, too: tarnished with fear. I lifted my head and looked at her: now, just as then, she was hugging herself, pulling her sleeves inward, cocooning herself in a disheveled shell.

"You know, too?" I asked before I could think to restrain myself, think through the situation. "You know about the person in the woods? The one with the red jacket?"

She stared back at me a little blankly. It was her natural look, the parted mouth, the loose cheeks, the slightly furrowed forehead. I'd seen her with that look on her face walking the corridors, sitting in class, running about in gym. A vapid expression sitting square on her face. Her natural look.

"I thought only I knew," I went on. "I didn't think anyone else was suspicious or connecting the dots. It was like my own terrible secret—" I stopped myself. For a brief second, she seemed incredulous. But then she shifted her head slightly, and a shaft of blue light blazed into my eyes. Her face disappeared into a corona of blue haze.

There was a long pause, a bloated, paralyzed moment. From somewhere within the nimbus of blue, she spoke in a husky whisper. "You can tell me your secrets."

I paused, thinking what to ask—but just then, the auditorium door opened at the far end. Framed within the doorway against the harsh light was the silhouette of two figures.

"Oh, the lights are off! It's pitch black in here." I recognized the voice. Zach Mayo, captain of the varsity soccer team, sought after by just about every girl who dared. "Where's the light switch?"

There was a girly giggle. "No, leave it off. It's better this way." It was Mindy Burns, widely rumored to have made out with at least half the senior jocks. She giggled again as the door swung shut behind them. "Let's go to the stage. There's a little light there."

I glanced at Jan Blair; she had also hunkered down under the lower railing. We were both partially hidden, visible only to the observant but not casual eye.

Zach Mayo and Mindy Burns came down the center aisle slowly, holding hands. In front of the stage, he placed his hands under her arms and lifted her onto the stage. She laughed in a frilly manner. He then pendulumed his body around, swinging his feet onto the stage like a gymnast scoring a perfect ten.

Mindy Burns passed under us as she walked to the back of the stage. Had she looked up, she would have seen us. Zach followed her. "Where are you going?" he asked. But it didn't seem like he was asking out of curiosity. There was a wicked smile on his face, a leer.

"Come back here and find out," she whispered. They apparently knew what was going to happen, because there was no further conversation. He simply went to her and wrapped his arms around her, bending her down gently onto the hardwood floor of the stage.

I heard him say, "Lynn's gonna kill me if she finds out." But Mindy started making sounds, and he didn't say anything more.

I was in a precarious position. All Mindy had to do was open her eyes and she would have seen me gaping at her. But then I felt a little warm breath on my nose. "Let's make our own secret," I heard Jan Blair whisper wetly. I raised my head and felt her lips suddenly grip around mine with verdant determination. Felt the sandpaper rash of acne at the corner of her mouth rubbing against my upper lip. Before I could move away, I felt her tongue—

Imagine that. Jan Blair, of all people.

It was dark by the time Mr. Matthewman let me out of practice. He was unhappy with me, grumbled that I was distracted. I was. He finally slammed the piano lid down in frustration.

"You're not here today," he grumbled. "I mean, you're here, but you're not *here*."

I started to protest, but he shook his head. "Just go to the library, will you—the town library."

"Why?"

"Go there and listen to some CDs. Listen to how some of the greats performed. Maybe you'll catch some of their passion. Pavarotti. Zancanaro. Nucci. Now go."

Inside Prattson Town Library, I headed for the CD section in the rear. I was halfway through my fourth CD—Mr. Matthewman was right, it was mesmerizing stuff—when something odd caught my attention: a small cluster of girls whispering intensely in one of the darkened, more isolated aisles. I recognized them—three seniors, very popular and with overrated beauty. They were the type who took a kind of sick pleasure in taunting the socially awkward, and I'd seen them inflicting cruel jokes on freshman girls. Something about their demeanor instantly grabbed me—the urgency in their eyes, a restlessness about the ways their fingers and hands flickered up and down. Their heads were locked together as if drawn in by a reverse centrifugal force, their voices hushed.

It was easy for me to make my way over without being noticed. I grabbed an index card, hastily scribbled something down, and made to look as if I were looking for a book. I went down the long aisle behind them, separated by a long stack shelved with enough books to offer me some cover. I ambled towards them, knowing with a dry certainty that I'd be unobserved. It was an art of mine, an ability to blend in. In a crowded room, on the street corner, loitering at a movie theater, I'd learned how to liquefy, to dissolve into the background. Their voices became clearer as I drew closer.

"...couldn't seem to get rid of him."

"Oh my God, like, you should have called me!"

"I don't know, I wasn't thinking straight, like, I was so freaked out."

"Are you sure you didn't recognize him...?"

"No, I told you he looked kinda familiar, but I just don't think...I don't really know..."

"And you said you—"

"I saw him standing outside my window for, like, ten minutes! Every time I peeked out between the curtains, there he was!"

Then the third voice, quiet until then, spoke: "The same thing happened to me."

There was a momentary pause.

I took two steps closer.

"What? Shut up!"

"Last...last week, I think it was Wednesday or Thursday. After cheerleading practice. Short person. Couldn't quite see who it was very clearly. Just like you. Followed me home."

"No!"

"Stood on the other side of the street, just watching the house."

"Why didn't you tell someone?"

"I did. I mean I was about to, but just when I'd made up my mind, he was gone. Like, just disappeared."

"Maybe we should—"

"Shh!"

A librarian walked up to them at that point, glaring. "This is not gossip central. This is a library. You'll either sit yourselves down with books to read, or leave."

The girls took off, too perturbed to put up any kind of fight. The librarian watched after them, suspicious.

I stayed for a couple of hours, not wanting to go back home, until almost closing. On the way out, I set off the book detector. It shrilled accusingly for a few seconds before cutting out. Libraries are supposed to be quiet, but in the following moments there was an altogether different kind of hush. Heads turned to stare, wariness rimming their gazes. The old men by the newspaper carrels, peered at me through their thick glasses; the librarians were all suddenly conscious of me, eyes turned to me from the corners of cagey eyes and half-turned heads. Naomi would tell me that I was being paranoid, that most folks simply didn't see me the way I thought they did. But she did not understand because, although Asian, she was a girl, and so did not live under the constant shadows of Fu Manchu, Seung-Hui Cho, and Long Duk Dong.

I felt eyes crawling over my body, snaking along my arm to the heavy backpack, to my hair, to a resemblance they believed was there. "It's OK," a librarian finally said, and I wasn't sure if she was speaking to me or to the other library patrons.

I tore out of the library, swearing never to return. Suddenly, I wanted to see Naomi. It was already late, but her home was on the way back. Kind of.

The house was already dark. Not even the flickering lights of a television. Her parents, exhausted after a long day, were likely already in bed. I sneaked around to the backyard, careful to avoid any fallen branches that might give me away. Her bedroom was on the second floor facing the backyard. A sturdy oak tree grew just outside, its branches thick and elongated, almost touching her window. I'd climbed that tree a thousand times before, usually late at night to give or receive a good book, homework, or some snacks through her window. Since her parents' bedroom was right next door and within earshot, we'd never dared talk aloud or even in whispers. We'd pass notes, each madly scribbling on a notepad. But that seemed a long time ago. The tree tonight seemed much smaller now, the footholds offering less traction as I climbed.

She wasn't asleep, just sitting at the foot of her bed with the lights off. She was in her pajamas, a pink, flimsy thing. She must have just combed her hair because it was set straight in tight lines. Her legs were tucked up against her chest, her chin resting up against her kneecaps, her arms wrapped tightly around her skinny legs. She was quietly sobbing.

I was about to tap on her window when I paused. In the movies, the dashing lead always knows what to say and do, knows how to provide the perfect antidote to tears with panache. But I didn't know the words, didn't know the actions. I placed my fingertips lightly on the windowpane.

Time passed. She was motionless inside, so stationary I thought she'd fallen asleep sitting up. But then she lay down. I hunkered deeper into the darkness of the tree, not wanting to be seen.

She covered herself with a blanket and faced the window. Tears lacquered her cheekbones. I stared, dreading the day when she'd fully realize the extent of her beauty. When she would walk past me on some ritzy Ivy League campus linked arm-in-arm with her to-die-for, drop-dead-handsome boyfriend, disregarding me in my (at honest best) SUNY Farmingdale sweatshirt with a casual flip of her hair, her eyes passing around and through me as if I were transparent.

For a few minutes, she continued to gaze out into darkness, still unaware that I was perched in the blackened foliage. Her pencil-brushed face, her tragic eyes. And before long, she drifted off to sleep, a calm settling upon her. I stayed on the tree limb long after her eyes remained closed, until her mouth parted, until her breathing steadied, softened. Only after I was sure she was asleep did I think about leaving.

But not immediately. I stayed on the tree even as the temperature dropped, even as the first snowflakes began their ghostly, shy descent. Because I wanted to.

DECEMBER 2

A jitteriness settled even deeper into Ashland, calcifying into a brittle fear. The school, taking note of the somber mood in the classrooms, brought in professional counselors. Mr. Marsworth ordered a mandatory counseling session for each student.

Over the course of the week, students were called at various times of the day for a private session, and soon it seemed that just about everyone had gone except me. Then, on a Friday afternoon, with only five minutes to go before school ended, I got the call to go. The school secretary walked in with a piece of paper in hand. She handed it wordlessly to Miss Winters, who walked over to me.

"Kris," she murmured tiredly, "it's your turn."

He was in classroom 258. Written on his face was the weary expression of a man cloistered too long in solitary confinement. On his desk was an open briefcase, files tossed haphazardly in. He was getting ready to leave.

"The other room," he said without looking up, pointing across the hallway.

I looked down at the piece of paper. "It says two fifty-eight."

"It's a mistake. Next door, please."

"It says two fifty-eight," I insisted. "I think you're the one who's mistaken."

For the first time he looked at me. "Do you now?"

"Yes. I have a note that says I'm supposed to meet with you here. Now."

"Give it to me." He grabbed it out of my hand, then sighed. "Well," he said loudly, "why don't you have a seat, then?"

I sat down.

"You want something to drink? Water? Soda?"

The trashcan next to the desk overflowed with used paper cups. I shook my head.

"So," he said, scratching a graying patch of hair just above his ear. "So." His eyes were bloodshot with fatigue. He cleared his throat and spoke louder, as if starting over. "Looking forward to the weekend?"

"I guess so."

"I'm sure by now your teachers have filled you in on what this is all about. No doubt your friends have let you in on what these counseling sessions are like. Right off the bat, er, Kris," he said, looking down at his notes, "I want you to know that this isn't an inquiry or an investigation at all. Some of the earlier students were under that mistaken impression. No, it's nothing more than a getting-to-know-you kind of get-together. We just want to know that you're doing OK."

I nodded. Outside, the bell rang, clanging with insistence that the week had ended and the weekend had begun. Within seconds, the clamor of voices and yelps of laughter broke out in the hallways.

"Have you been sleeping OK? Your appetite doing all right? These are the usual symptoms of what we call event stress or event tension." His sleeves were rolled up unevenly, arm hair tufting out as if for air.

He asked a host of questions in so mechanical a fashion that I began to suspect that he was merely running down a list. He barely seemed interested in or responsive to what I was saying.

Then something changed, barely perceptible, in the tone of his voice, in the posture of his form. His eyes lingered on mine just that much longer—sharper, harder. I continued to answer as best I could: no, I was not good friends with either Justin Dorsey or Winston Barnes; no, I hadn't talked with either of them on the day of the disappearance; no, I hadn't seen anything unusual around school.

And then it hit me. This was no counselor in front of me. This was a person pretending to be a counselor. His questions were just all wrong. His initial questions were right on target—those a counselor would typically ask—but the questions he was asking now seemed more investigatory, something a detective might ask. His were questions seeking a breakthrough, hoping to expose. I studied him carefully. No, not a counselor—he had *undercover* written all over him. My mind started to race. Did they really suspect the killer was a *student*, as Naomi had theorized?

He rubbed his chin. "It says here that you've gone through some counseling before." The question hung in the air like an unused ceiling fan.

I sat up slightly, arms crossed. "Is that what this is? An official counseling session?"

"Not really. Not that formal. Just a chance to chat." He fingered the papers in front of him. "But let's get back to your past. You've had professional counseling before?"

"Well, yes. Some years back."

"And what was that about?"

I gave an aw-shucks grin. "Just something silly. Just me being a kid."

"What was it all about?"

"What is *this* all about?" I asked, and he flicked his eyes up to meet mine.

He tapped his clipboard once, twice. "Back then, your teachers thought you should get some therapy, it says here."

"That's right. I did get some therapy."

He crossed his legs. "What kind of therapy?"

"Not sure. Something to do with my imagination."

"Your teachers thought it was overactive?" he asked, his forefinger lining a few words.

"It's what they thought. But it was nothing."

"No?"

"No."

His eyes studied mine carefully. "Your imagination was overactive. Specifically, how?"

"I mean, like I said. It was nothing."

"Hmm," he murmured, but his eyes were very alert now. "It says here…" he glanced down at his notes, "that you came to this country seven years ago."

"That's about right."

He leaned back in his chair and uncrossed his legs, only to cross them again quickly. "With your family," he said.

"With my family."

"With your parents, right? You don't have any siblings?"

"Right."

He shuffled through a few papers again, this time a little slower. "And you went through counseling shortly after your father passed away?"

I looked down at my hands. "That's right."

"And how did he…?" He leafed through more papers on his clipboard.

"A traffic accident. Driver hit and killed my father. I couldn't sleep for a long time after. I was having difficulty at school. They said I was imagining things, weird things. So I went through counseling."

"And how did that go?"

"I'm here, aren't I? I'm alive, right?"

A frown crossed his face. "How long did the counseling last?"

"A couple of months or so."

"What was the problem?"

"There was no problem."

"You said there was something about your imaginat—"

"It was a *grief mechanism*," I cut in, "a kind of *wish fulfillment*. That's what they called it. I would imagine that my father was around, even after his death." I did not elaborate. I did not mention—as I once had to the grief counselor—how vivid those encounters had been, whole afternoons my dead father and I spent together. It was the only way I could cope with the pain. "The counseling ended after only a few sessions. That was a long time ago."

"But I see here that your grades took a hit. Even put on academic probation for a while." He looked at me as if he expected some kind of response. "And you started acting out, playing truant from school for a spell as well, I see that here."

"Guilty as charged," I said, smirking now with my arms raised in surrender.

He stared hard into my eyes. "Right." Then, looking away, he mumbled perfunctorily, "I'm sorry for your loss."

"It was years ago."

"Yes." He eyes returned to his notes, his eyebrows furrowing. "I see also that your mother had counseling?"

"Yes, she did."

"For depression," he said. "And this was for a few months." *Should have been for a few years.* "Yes."

"And she was prescribed medication, Prozac?"

"Yes." *Until money ran out.*

"And she's fine now?"

"Dandy. Positively perky. Not a cloud over her head. She motivates me every day, she's a real force."

He flipped the clipboard onto the desk, his eyes taking a quick peek at his watch. "Well, OK, I just want to be sure you're doing fine. In light of recent events."

"Just fine."

"Any loss of appetite?"

"Nope."

"Sleeping problems?"

"Nope."

"Distracted? Hard to focus on things?"

"What did you say?"

"No?"

"No. Just fine."

"Very good," he said, snapping his file shut. "I think we're just about done here."

I hesitated in my seat. There was something I wanted to ask him, and it must have shown: he asked if anything was the matter.

"No," I said, shaking my head. I got up to leave.

"Have a good weekend, OK, kiddo?"

I slung my backpack over my shoulder and went to the door. I turned to him again. "You know, I was wondering…" I shook my head. "Nah, it's nothing."

"No, what is it?"

"It just that…has anyone looked into the red jacket?"

"Red jacket?" His hands, busy throwing files into his briefcase, paused.

"Yeah. When Winston Barnes went nuts in class, he kept talking about being followed by someone in a red jacket. I'm just wondering if the cops followed up on that."

"Winston Barnes said he was followed by a someone in a red jacket?"

I nodded. "I was just wondering if that happened to anyone else. Being followed by someone wearing a red jacket."

He was looking warily at me now. "Have you heard something?"

"I mean, this school is gossip central. Everything—*everything*—gets talked about. Maybe some other students heard stuff?"

"What have you heard?" The pencil he'd been twirling had fallen to the desk, forgotten.

I could have told him right there about being chased through the woods. About the red jacket I'd seen. It was on the tip of my tongue to say something. But instead I just shrugged. "Everyone's got their pet theory. The red-jacket theory, the blue-dog theory, the black-car theory, the rainbow—" I stood up, grabbed my things. "I mean, I could tell you all of them, but it'll take at least twenty minutes."

He paused, studying me for a second. Then he shook his head, sighing. "No, we're done here."

MOTHER

After my father's death, my mother's fall into depression had been immediate and deep. There was no gradual sinking into a pool of sadness; this was a plunge, with sandbags and weights tied around her ankles, into cold blackness.

Kai Gong! Kai Gong! Her voice, hysterical like a little girl's, calling out for her husband along the dark empty road. Her son behind her, shaking his head, his chest hitching.

Kai Gong! Kai Gong! Her shrieks, the naked scream of the violated, slicing leaves off branches. Her hands, cradling his bloodied head. Her eyes shut in denial, her mouth opened in an endless scream. The lights of neighboring homes turned on, faces pressed against windows, too frightened to come out towards the strange, foreign screams. And then the ambulance arrived, swallowing up my father behind clanging doors. And still my mother screaming, *Kai Gong! Kai Gong!* The sound still haunts me.

About a month after my father's death, I woke up in the middle of the night. The house was silent, as it had been for weeks, as if the silence of my father's coffin had stolen into this house. I was thirsty and crept downstairs for some water. I was about to enter the kitchen when I sensed someone there.

It took only a second to see it was my mother. She was sitting at the breakfast table, back to me, her legs cradled up against her chest. She was embracing them as if shimmying up a tree. Perfectly still, more mannequin than human. I caught her face in the mirror, her taut skin stretched over her softly protruding cheekbones. She had been beautiful in her youth, my father used to tell me, proudly. She filled the home in China with laughter, he used to say, and there was always a wicked shine in her eyes. That was the way she had once been, before the crossing to America.

Her downturned eyes, reflected in the mirror, were now cauldrons of pain. In my counseling sessions, I'd been told that suffering was never pleasant; but even the bloodiest and most excruciating of wounds would in time heal. I looked at my crumpled mother. Hers was something else. It was a wound that would never heal, only bleed in newer and rawer places over time.

I was hidden in the shadows as I stepped towards her. For some reason, I stopped. Perhaps I would have said, *"Ah-ma,"* and put my hand on her shoulder, and she would have turned around and embraced me. Perhaps. But I stood frozen behind her.

Then she sensed me. For a long time she didn't say anything. She sniffed hard but kept quiet, possibly hoping that I would just leave. She didn't want me to see her like this, eyes smeared over with grief. But I didn't leave, and she finally said, "Please go back to bed, Xing."

"Are we returning to China?" I asked.

"No," she said with a soft finality.

"Why not?"

"Because we have no choice. Because we have to stay. Because of you."

I did not understand what she meant. And then I felt it for the first time, the silent accusation taking shape, a hideous presence that would never completely leave my life.

"Now go back to bed," she said.

My answer came many seconds later in quavering yet resolute words. It was all new to her when I said in English, "Yes, Mother." I never called her *Ah-ma* again.

At school, I was taught that you can't really feel your heart beating inside, not even when you're scared or have just run hard. You can feel only the pumping of blood; the heart itself, that muscular organ, can't be felt. And how true. Because that night, as I made my way slowly back up the stairs, I felt nothing inside me. Nothing at all.

DECEMBER 5

I awoke with a start. Night. Cold. The house silent.

I got up and went to the window. My mother was home, the car parked in the driveway under a deepening layer of snow. Delicate flakes softly peppered the window. A cast of mercury moonlight spread over the homes, the streetlamps, the cars, the lawns. I loved this time of night, when the house was dark and quiet, when the neighborhood was asleep and unaware. When it seemed like I alone in the world was awake.

Very softly, I began to sing. My breath frosted the windowpane.

There were three hesitant knocks on my door.

They startled me—I hadn't heard any approaching footsteps in the hallway outside. I turned around, staring at the door, doubting my ears.

Knock. Knock. Knock.

They came not from the door, but from the wall, right above my bed. Three gentle, almost apologetic knocks from the other side of the wall. Miss Durgenhoff.

There was a long pause, and then, once again, three knocks.

I tiptoed over to the wall and hunkered down. I pressed my ear against the wall, unable to shake the impression that she was doing the same on the other side, our ears separated only by the thinnest of barriers. I waited, and I sensed her waiting, too.

When I could take it no longer, I whispered, "Yes?"

And her voice came back almost immediately, muffled from the other side. "Can I come over?"

She came in with a tray of crackers and two cups of green tea. "Just in case you're hungry," she said.

We ate the crackers silently, soft crackers which broke easily in the mouth. I sipped at the tea and felt warmth cascade down my throat.

"You have quite a remarkable voice," she said, breaking the silence.

"I thought I've been singing quietly. Have I been waking you?"

"Nonsense, child. Sleep comes fleetingly at my age, in little snippets. I don't so much sleep anymore as take multiple catnaps throughout the day and night." She looked around the room. "It's a little bare, don't you think?"

"Well, it's the way I like it."

"A teenage boy should have more sports paraphernalia, swimsuit posters, stuff—" She came to an abrupt stop as her eyes came upon the painting. "My, my, my. Now that's an interesting painting." She stood up to take a closer look.

"It's just a painting."

"Yes, but…" She craned her neck forward, scrutinizing the painting.

"It's just a painting," I repeated. "Somebody painted it for me once."

"A long time ago?"

"Not really."

"It's of China, isn't it? Somewhere you know?"

It was a painting of the village where I was born. My father had painted it for me just weeks before he was killed. On many nights, I would lie awake gazing at it. The village fields, the mountains rising in the distance like shy ghosts. The sun bleeding into the sea. The sampans caught in the fiery blaze of the reflected sunset. My childhood home tucked into the corner, the terraced fields tumbling down. The painting would fill me with a sadness as I drifted off to sleep and awaken me with deep longing in the morning. It could do that to me—arouse feelings in me that adults triple my age only read about. It was a painting that confounded me as much as it soothed. "It's my hometown," I said. "My father painted it."

She absorbed my words thoughtfully, then turned to the window. "The snow outside. So pretty. Like petals of a flower falling." She smiled at me. Nobody looked at me the way she did or registered my words as deeply as she.

"I've been hearing you sing quite a bit recently." She smiled again. "The wall between us is rather thin. Are you preparing for something? Or just singing for enjoyment?"

"There's a musical my school's putting on."

"And you have a lead role?"

"Not exactly?"

"A secondary role, surely, then. The songs you sing don't sound like a chorus number."

"Well, I actually don't have any role. I'm the understudy."

"Seems a shame for one as talented as yourself to be warming the bench. Who's got the lead, Pavarotti?"

"Ha. This kid Anthony Hasbourd has the lead. Every year he gets the lead."

"Sounds like he must be quite the singer."

I shook my head. "His mother is the head of the PTA or something like that, has a lot of clout, and flexes her muscles every year to get her son the lead. He's good enough that most people don't mind."

"And but for him, you'd have the role."

I shrugged. "I don't know. I suppose."

We watched the snow falling outside.

"It's very quiet here," she said finally. "Took some getting used to for me. In the beginning."

I nodded.

"You mom's quiet, too, when she's home. Just in her room with the television on."

I could feel her eyes turn to me, not unkindly.

She shook her head, as if reprimanding herself. "Anyway, all this just to say that I'm glad you've been singing. Every time you sing, I perk up a little. Breaks up some of the quiet around here." She smacked her lips in self-agreement.

I pulled my pillow over, propping it under my armpit. I saw her gaze back at the painting.

"A remarkable painting, really," she said, squinting intensely. "Your father was very gifted. You can tell he loved his art. Look at the textured strokes, the incredible use of light, the spacing. Very special." She turned to look at me. "Do you know how to tell whether a painting is special or not, Kris?"

I shook my head.

"There are always two levels to a painting—a good painting, anyway. There is the surface painting—what is immediately obvious to the eye. But then there is the secret painting lying underneath. Aim for that, Kris, to see beyond the surface. All great paintings have it, a hidden layer. A secret painting."

"A secret painting?"

She nodded.

I stared at the painting. "I don't see it."

She smiled.

We were quiet for a few minutes. Outside, flakes fell silently, gently accumulating on the windowsill. The radiator hissed; then it sighed heavily and shuddered to an end. A hush enveloped us.

"Tell me," she said in a near whisper, "something about your life in China."

"What would you like to hear?"

She thought for a few moments. "Tell me about your home. Your family. The school you went to. Your friends. Tell me what you did on summer nights. Tell me some of your happiest memories."

I looked at the painting, then back at her. "That would take a long time."

She smiled. "I have all night."

DECEMBER 10

On December 10, Anthony Hasbourd disappeared. These are the undisputed facts. He arrived at school a few minutes late, his appearance a little disheveled but nothing out of the ordinary. What *was* odd about his behavior, however, was his constant agitation. Classmates noticed he couldn't seem to sit still. His eyes bugged out, swiveling back and forth. He was nervous. And incredibly fatigued. During study hall, he kept nodding asleep, the bags under his eyes lumpy and swollen.

In the hysteria that broke out after his disappearance, it was difficult to separate fact from fiction. There was talk about Hasbourd locking himself in a bathroom stall, sobbing and crying. Rumors of how he was seen running down the corridor as if being chased. What is known for sure is that during French class he had asked the teacher if he could go to the restroom. He walked out the door, and that was the last time he was seen.

The only thing recovered was his left boot. It was found just outside the main entrance, at the foot of a sign announcing the winter musical: *The Man from Jerusalem*—starring Anthony Hasbourd. Befuddled police took photographs of the boot and stood with coffee cups in gloved hands, sipping.

Parents were in a furor over the disappearance. A few began to keep their children home altogether. Most began carpooling their kids, and the roads were now rife with traffic early in the morning and late afternoon. Any outsider found walking on school grounds during the day was immediately surrounded by security guards. Reporters (and more were trickling in by the week) were under strict instructions not to trespass onto school grounds and to refrain from interviewing any of the students traveling to and from school.

Two days later, Anthony Hasbourd still hadn't been found. It was a gray Thursday morning when Mr. Matthewman finally broached the topic neither one of us had dared bring up.

"The show's continuing. You have the lead now."

I sat on the piano stool, stunned.

"What about——?"

"We've been discussing it nonstop. Consulted with the Hasbourds. The teachers, Mr. Marsworth, we all got together last night for a long meeting. We think it's the right thing to do. It's what," he said perfunctorily, "Anthony would want."

"Really?" I asked incredulously.

He nodded. "It wasn't actually that hard, convincing them to go on with the show. We all think it's good for the other students, keeps morale up, keeps their minds preoccupied with things other than the disappearances. What was harder," he said, turning his eyes away from mine, "was convincing them that you should be the lead now. That you're good enough."

I pushed down lightly and arbitrarily on some of the piano keys in front of me. They made a discordant, jangled sound. "They thought you were joking at first?"

He sighed then shook his head apologetically. "When they saw that I was serious, one of the teachers said he didn't think you could even speak English."

I brought my elbows down onto the piano keys and ran my hands through my hair. I stared at the worn-out keys.

"I know it must hurt you, Kris, to hear that."

"You must have had to fight tooth and nail for me."

"Some. But not so much. The show's become a political thing now. Too many bigwigs have put their names behind it; others are waiting to jump on the bandwagon. It's going to happen. And with the performance less than a fortnight away, there's no time to start from scratch with someone else. So you slip right in."

I lifted my head. "I wish you'd asked me first. I might not want to do this."

"And that's exactly why I didn't ask you first."

I stood up slowly from the piano and took a step away. "The early morning lessons and everything were, you know, great and all," I said. "But I guess I never really thought about it. I wanted the part, but now that I have it, I don't know anymore."

"Most people have no inkling how good you are, that, really, you kill him." He reached for his coffee mug and took a thoughtful sip. "Bad choice of words. But you have a talent the likes of which I've seen only at Julliard. You're raw, there's no doubt about that, but you're truly gifted."

"You think I can sing? Like *really* sing?"

He smiled a little. "I've been wrong on many things before. But not this one. You can sing, Kris."

"I can sing?"

"I didn't want to tell you unless you got the lead. You'll make the angels stop and listen."

Later, as I walked down the hallway, my head swam in a pool of adrenaline. The world spun faster, somehow brighter. I zipped into homeroom exhilarated and took my seat. It all looked the same to me—disinterested students hunched over desks, slouched shoulders—but something in me was burning hot and fierce. Naomi must have noticed. She kept eyeing me, sensing something was very different, that something momentous had just occurred. I turned and flashed her the most winsome of smiles. Her eyes widened in disbelief.

My voice lessons with Mr. Matthewman immediately kicked into high gear. Every morning now, before even the crack of dawn, I arose, dressed silently, and left the house. But something felt different about the streets now. For weeks, I had enjoyed the stillness, the absolute solitude of early dawn. But now the empty roads and sleeping homes seemed to hum with a hidden danger, to be closing in on me like a noose.

Mr. Matthewman seemed oddly uninterested in the commotion seizing the town. If he had any feelings at all, he never voiced them. All he seemed interested in, from the moment I stepped into the music room, was my singing. The time was getting near, he would say, coughing into his hand, always getting nearer with too much to do, too much to practice. "Now," he would typically say even before I'd taken off my backpack, "shall we begin with C major scale?"

Like chiseling a statue out of hardened marble, Mr. Matthewman slowly cropped me into shape. I remember how he would stoop low as he listened to me from his piano stool, his dissecting ear leaned towards me, sometimes so close that I could see the swirls of white and gray hair protruding from the canal.

He proved to be a stickler for scientific explanations, going into depth about the bodily intricacies involved in the act of singing. "Exhale slowly as you sing through a long phrase, Kris, as if to make your breath warm and wet. Feel that muscle? That's the epigastric muscle. Never let it loosen up on you—don't suck it in as you tease out the last notes of the verse, or you'll lose your breath. Move in too quickly with your epigastric, and your diaphragm is going to collapse on you, and—*zip!*—just like that, your breath is gonna get plugged up. Keep it firm and steady," he'd say, nodding his head quickly up and down like the spindle of an inverted loom, "like that feeling when you first inhale your first full breath."

Occasionally, the significance of these practices, the enormity of having the lead role, would bowl me over. Mr. Marsworth defended publically his decision to continue with the show. In a statement that was later quoted extensively by national media outlets, he "preached resilience in the face of adversity and a determination not to be swayed by the whims of a depraved murderer." The musical, he said, would render a sense of normalcy to the kids; it would show the town that life went on; it would be a healthy detractor from all the brouhaha. Most of the community bought into it.

And involvement in the show took on a sort of moral badge. New duties were created: stage director, publicity coordinator, lighting manager, and other titles full of self-importance but signifying nothing. Funding poured in for stage design and costumes, and the chorus, once considered maxed out at twenty-five students, was expanded to accommodate forty. A local print shop offered its services for free: it would use expensive, glossy paper to produce posters for the show, and navy blue lined paper for the programs.

It was never in dispute that the poster had to be changed. Anthony Hasbourd's face was in the foreground of the original, his blue eyes blazing like simmering coals from his cherubic face. The poster was completely redesigned by a professional designer. It was a wonderful design in the end, sophisticated but not pretentious, colorful and eye-catching but not overdone. I was never asked to pose for the poster, never asked to give a photograph of myself. Only Mr. Matthewman gave me a straight explanation, albeit after much prodding. The school had decided not to feature me on the poster because I bore, in their eyes, an eerie resemblance to Seung-Hui Cho, the Virginia Tech killer. In fact, many thought I was his spitting image.

I look nothing like him.

And so I wandered the hallways undisturbed, skulked in the classrooms, loitered in the library, never bothered. The fame and attention I'd assumed were part and parcel with being the lead were proving to be elusive. Around me, there was ceaseless activity on a production of which I was the centerpiece; but with the exception of just a few curious looks thrown my way, nobody seemed to take much note of me at all. I was the invisible and mute commander of a gigantic army, still unheard, unseen, insignificant.

DECEMBER 18

I was lackluster, and Mr. Matthewman sensed it right from the get-go. He bore it as long as he could, then he tapped his fingers impatiently on his thigh.

"What's the matter today, Kris?" he asked. "You seem a little out of sorts. Distracted."

"Nothing. Just a little tired, I guess."

He nodded as if to himself. "I had a conversation with some of the teachers yesterday. They wanted to know when you were going to sing with the chorus. They've been getting nervous with so much riding on this musical, so much money being poured in, extra media coverage now." He pushed down a few stray strands of hair that had risen up antenna-like. "So I've arranged for you to meet with the rest of the chorus at tonight's rehearsal. It's time, Kris. The show's only five days away, after all."

"I don't think I'm ready," I stammered. "I need to practice more—"

Mr. Matthewman interrupted. "I thought about it. But there's only so much, you know what I'm talking about? After a while, you just got to do it. Stand up. Sing. In front of them."

I stood very quietly, very still. It was sinking in. "How many people will there be?"

"For tonight, just the chorus. Forty of them. The orchestra. Plus all the teachers involved. The principal."

"So about eighty people?"

"Yes."

Eighty. The number seemed astronomical. A whole clan, a tribe, a whole town. Eighty people, all their eyes trained on me. "That's a lot of people."

"Yes."

"I've never formally performed before. Not before a single person."

"I'm a person."

"You don't count."

"I've been told that before," he said wryly.

"You know what I mean." I fidgeted with my wristwatch. "I just think I need more time."

"Confidence. You need more confidence, not time. I guarantee you, you get more confidence, and you'll bust through the stratosphere. And the only way to get more confidence is to perform in front of people."

I shuffled a little on my feet, then made my way to my backpack sitting in the corner. I placed my music sheets carefully inside.

"Have you heard anything new about Anthony?" I asked, trying to change the topic. I thought he might know something, being a teacher and all.

He shook his head. "Nothing. With all the media coverage, usually something turns up. But nothing in this case at all."

"I suppose zilch on Barnes, too?"

He nodded, sighing heavily. "Gone without a trace. It's eerie." He coughed into his hand. "It's been on all our minds.

I know you've been concerned. Listen," he said, piling the music sheets atop the piano, "I've already kept you over. I've been pushing you too much lately. Let's end here." He winked at me, a cavalier attitude he rarely displayed. "We've been going at it for weeks. Rest up for tonight."

I hoisted my backpack on. "What time?" I asked.

"Five."

"Eighty people?"

He nodded. "Just remember you don't have to prove yourself. You've already done that time and again. Just be yourself."

I didn't want to tell him this, but nothing was less reassuring to me than when someone told me to just be myself. "OK," I replied, "five it is."

★

On account of my longer practice with Mr. Matthewman that morning, I missed homeroom, but I made it to my first period class, math. I almost stumbled into Jan Blair's desk.

Since the day Jan Blair kissed me, I'd been bedeviled by the thought that she might start treating me like a boyfriend. All kinds of scenarios played themselves out during sleepless nights: she'd sit waiting at my seat, scrawling *I luv Kris* all over her hand, or she'd follow me around school like a sick puppy. But for the most part I found her to be her usual drab self, much like this morning, sitting at her desk, a faraway look in her eyes.

Naomi was at her desk, too, writing furiously. I took my seat next to her.

"Maybe we should…" she muttered as if to herself.

"What?"

"Maybe we should have dinner together at the food court tonight." She said this while still writing in her journal, not looking at me. "It's been, like, forever since we've hung out. My parents are trying out a new eggplant dish. I've told them that white folks don't like eggplant, but they're very insistent."

"Tonight may not be good. I have a rehearsal. Mr. Matthewman just told me."

She stopped writing and looked at me finally. "We haven't been able to talk, hardly, anymore. In the morning you no longer take the bus. After school you're off doing some singing lessons again. We're kind of losing touch."

"It's not just my fault. I'm free on the weekends, but you're off doing your own stuff."

"It's church stuff. And it's important to me."

"Well, so is singing to me. This musical. There's all this pressure on me—I hardly have time to myself. And the performance is only five days away, and—" I stopped. I could see she wasn't in the mood for an argument.

"I have stuff going on in my life," she said.

Don't we all? I wanted to say.

"How about after your rehearsal? If you get let out early enough?"

"I can't. It's with the chorus, for the first time. It'll run late."

"OK. Whatever." She went back to her writing.

And then something terrible happened.

Jan Blair turned to Naomi and gave her a folded piece of paper. Naomi frowned at it, perplexed, then she quickly unfolded it and started to read.

"Pass it to Kris!" Jan Blair hissed. "It's a note for *him*, not you."

Naomi handed it to me with a quizzical expression.

I'm not one to turn red, but at that moment I could feel
the flush of heat hit my cheeks. I wanted to duck my head
into my turtleneck and never come out again. I grabbed the
note and rammed it unread into my pocket like used tissue.

Thankfully, Mr. Jefferson walked in at that moment. He
looked even more tired than usual. Rumor had it he was going through an ugly divorce and was losing custody of his
kids, all of which was taking a toll on him. He was also a
lousy teacher, never interacting with students, giving out
only multiple-choice homework and tests. He sat with a weary groan and smoothed out some papers on his desk.

From outside the classroom, far down the hallway, a girl
started to laugh.

"All right," Mr. Jefferson said, "I have just a few announcements to make before we begin class." He looked up
to the back of the classroom and glared for a second before
clearing his throat a little too demonstrably. "Do you mind?
Can I have some quiet, please?"

And in that drawn-out moment when the classroom
quieted to a murmur, the girl's laughter rang out even more
clearly. It was one of those hysterical, out-of-control laughs.

All Mr. Jefferson did was shake his head. "All right," he
said, leafing through a pile of announcements, "first off, we
have an announcement about *The Man from Jerusalem*. The
school is asking for more volunteers to serve as car parking
attendees. Apparently we need to open up the soccer field to
accommodate yet even more guests. It will—" He stopped
right there, turning to the door. The girl's laughter was getting louder. He scratched his bald head with his pinkie finger, brushing aside wispy strands of hair. "As I was saying,"
he continued, but then the laughter broke an octave higher.
"As I was saying," he said again, but then he stopped again.
The laughter was even louder now. His face suddenly turned

scarlet, all the way up to the top of his head. "For cryin' out loud!" he crackled, livid, raising his fist to slam it down on the desktop. But then he froze.

The laughter outside suddenly screeched into a scream.

We all realized it, together, at that moment: it had never been laughter. The whole time, it had been one long, hysterical scream.

Mr. Jefferson looked at us as if for reassurance, or at least some direction. Then, coming to his senses, he bolted out of his chair and into the hallway. A few students tried to follow him, but he pointed them back in with a ferocious finger. Out in the corridor already, a few teachers were glancing nervously out of their classrooms, many with one foot in the door, one hand still fastened on the doorknob. The scream emanated from down the hallway in the east wing. From the girls' bathroom there.

For a long time, the screaming did not stop. Instead, it only seemed to get louder, shriller, to break into different pitches and amplitudes until it became apparent that there was more than one person screaming now. Loud shouts jostled with one another, masculine voices doddering in panic.

Inside my homeroom, a few of my classmates were already on their cell phones, frantically calling their parents. It was a classroom suddenly filled with trembling hands and the trilling of jumpy, panicky voices. A student sitting by the front wanted to place furniture against the door, to barricade us in.

"Somebody call the police," said Alexander Bonds from the front of the classroom with his baritone voice. "Somebody freakin' call the damn police." But by then, police cars with wailing sirens were already rushing towards school.

There would be no rehearsal that night.

───────── ★ ─────────

The school went into lockdown for a few hours. Nobody was allowed to leave the classrooms, not even to go to the restroom. SWAT teams came trooping in—we could hear the sound of their boots ricocheting along the hallways, the static of their walkie-talkies hissing in the relative quiet. We learned of what happened only in bits and pieces, mostly by text-messaging people on the outside. A severed hand had been found in one of the restrooms. No body. Yet. There was quite a bit of sobbing, some hugging. Naomi ignored me the whole time.

Then we watched as class after class was released. We'd all seen it before—Columbine, Virginia Tech—lines of students running out in single file, hands raised above their heads, expressions caught somewhere between fear and panic. What you don't see are the photographers, scores of them clicking away, their bulbs flashing, turning the whole spectacle into a weird catwalk of fear. Another thing you don't see is students falling, even though I witnessed at least five trip. I guess the media outlets have concluded it's bad form to show panicking, fear-stricken kids falling ungracefully on their rumps.

Then came our turn. Five SWAT officers came in, all with guns drawn. We were told to stand at our desks with our bags in front of us. They were going to search our bags and pat us down, just as a precaution.

Some years ago—was it in fifth or in sixth grade?—my teacher's wallet had gone missing. My teacher was an old pixie of a woman who spoke too fast, whose wiry white hair was never combed, and whose pinched, determined lips sat atop a pointed chin. The wallet had been placed carelessly on her desk; in the afternoon it disappeared. She'd gone ballistic and ordered us to put our backpacks in front of us.

She spent the longest time on my bag. I should have known. She went through other bags before getting to me, but she'd rifled through them almost perfunctorily. Mere patdowns, really. But when she'd gotten to mine, her fingers seemed to develop dirty talons.

She went through my things.

Suddenly every pocket seemed important to her; every zipper had to be unzipped. She spent roughly five seconds on each of the other bags; with mine, however, she'd spent at least a good minute. I sat reddening as if angry or embarrassed. But I was neither. I was stung.

I hadn't stolen her wallet. Nobody had so much as touched her wallet. I alone observed her later that day as she was putting on her coat. As her hand brushed by the coat pocket, she froze. I could see her fingers pressing against a bulging rectangular shape in her pocket. She'd pursed her lips. And never said a thing.

When the SWAT officer got to my desk, he asked me to turn and face the window. I complied. His gloved hands frisked me with efficiency; he was done before I knew it. Then he asked me to open my bag.

This, too, he went through with efficiency. He was about to move on to the next student, was really giving my bag just one last perfunctory squeeze...when he paused. Somehow his team members sensed something was off because within moments they were all surrounding the bag, surrounding me. He unzipped a side pocket.

"What do you have here, son?" he asked.

I said nothing.

He pulled out a gravity knife from the side pocket. "This yours, correct?"

I blinked. I'd never seen that knife before in my life. Never.

"Do you speak English?" He was opening the blade, examining it closely. The other officers closed in on me. The officer with the knife turned to Mr. Jefferson. "Does he speak—?"

"Of course he does," Naomi suddenly interjected. She was standing at the front of the classroom, in line with most of the other students, ready to run out. "What's the problem?"

"Are you his sister?"

"Of course not."

"Does he speak English?" he asked, pointing at me.

She turned to me, her eyes piercing me with anger and fear. "Kris, just say something."

And quite suddenly, every student lined up at the door was staring at me with a curious look. Some of them were frowning at me.

The officer turned to Mr. Jefferson. "Does he speak English?"

Mr. Jefferson paused. He was looking at me carefully now, as if seeing me for the first time. "I don't know," he said, and he turned to Naomi. "Does he?"

"I do," I finally said in a low whisper. "What's the problem?"

The officer's eyes were blue and cold, unsettling. "No problem," he said, and his voice had a quiet authority. He ordered the officers to finish up with the other students. They kept me standing as he went through my bag again, checking the lining, even the arm straps. Then they dismissed the line of students.

I watched as they ran across the yard. Nobody tripped.

"What's with the knife?" the officer asked.

"I don't know," I said. "I've never seen it before."

"You've never seen it before."

"No. I haven't."

"How did it get into your backpack?"

"Listen, I don't know. Honest to God, I've never seen it before. I'm just as surprised as you are."

"All right, turn around again. Hands on your head."

They frisked me again, more deliberately and thoroughly this time. But they found nothing else. After that, there wasn't much else they could do. In the end, they confiscated the knife, sealing it in an evidence bag, and took down my information. They fingerprinted me, too. My ten prints stared back at me like black eyes beaten down with accusation. Then they let me go, long after everyone else had left.

And so I was *completely* alone when I ran out of school, arms raised above my head as I'd been instructed. Just me. And maybe it was because, after seeing hoards of students running together all day, it was so unusual to see only one person running; but for whatever reason, the cameras broke into a blinding frenzy. Flashlights burst out all around me. Maybe they just thought, *What's with this Asian kid?* and decided to snap a few shots. Maybe they thought I was the killer making a break for it. Whatever the case, let me tell you, it felt truly magnificent to run out there all alone like some fugitive escapee, eyes wide like the proverbial deer in the headlights, almost peeing in my pants with fear, with all those cameras flashing away with renewed vigor. Just terrific. At least I didn't trip.

Naomi called me later that night. I told her everything was fine. No, the knife didn't belong to me. And no, I had no idea how it ended up in my backpack. I really didn't want to talk about it. I could tell she was holding back, that she wanted to be angry at me for the way I'd been so silent back in the classroom. It always infuriated her, how I'd just retreat into my shell. We didn't talk long, just enough for us both to realize that we'd fallen so out of touch. I sensed there was more that she really wanted to talk about.

The house was especially quiet that night. My mother wouldn't be home for at least a couple more hours, and Miss Durgenhoff was apparently asleep already. I climbed the staircase and sat down on my bed.

It was then that I remembered Jan Blair's note. It was tucked deep into my pocket, and I dug it out, moist and soft now, the ink diluted and wilted. Her handwriting was scratchy and razor-thin.

Come meet me at the my home. after midnite. cause I want to tell you sumthing. About our secret.

I crumpled the note into a ball. Then I reopened it and read it again. What Naomi had also read. Alone in my room, secluded from the rest of the world, even there I cringed in abject horror and embarrassment.

I almost didn't go. I practiced some of my songs, but it was a distracted, halfhearted hour of practice. I turned in early, around ten thirty, hoping that I'd fall quickly into a sound sleep. But instead I tossed and turned and tossed and turned until I found myself tossing my bike off its stand and turning around Fexter Street, towards Stillgate Street, over the bridge, and down a dirt road leading into the woods. Jan lived somewhere in there. An abandoned trailer, according to rumor. Nobody really knew.

It was further into the woods than I'd thought it would be. When it became too dark to navigate, I propped up my bike on its kickstand. With no light to guide me now, I walked tentatively forwards, farther into the darkness.

And just like that, I broke into a clearing. She didn't live in a trailer home, but she might as well have. A shack-like house sat in the clearing surrounded by debris; an acidic aroma hung about like a damp cloth.

Crouching low, I slunk along the tree line, my eyes trained on the shack. Even the moonlight seemed to want to shy away from this canker sore. I edged closer. No sign of life from within the house. The fetid aroma grew more pungent by the second.

Taking a deep breath, I stepped flush into the sickly moonlight, into the weedy clearing. My boots sank sickeningly into the ground as I scurried across it and onto the rickety porch. A bench cross-hatched with cracks was keeled over like a drunk. I stood outside the front door, listening. Not a sound.

Perhaps I'd been all wrong about this, misinterpreted what Jan Blair had written. Or perhaps I wasn't even at her residence but the home of a lunatic hobo. I inched my way to the window and peered in. A filthy sheet hung against the window, giving away nothing of what lay within. I made my way back to the door. A second later, I turned to leave but then found myself nudging the door with my finger. The door, light as a leaf, creaked open. I stared into the interior darkness, moonlight nudging in.

Even in the cold of night, the inside of the shack stank of sweat in all the wrong places. A few cans of fish lay opened and discarded on a table, a splattering of utensils around them. A furry creature sat on the table, astride one of the opened cans, licking. A cat. Its eyes gazed at me with a faint glow.

I stood very still. From somewhere towards the back of the room came the slight *puff* of a snore pushed between blubbery lips. Then a wheezy intake of breath, a violin played out of tune. Judging from the volume of the snore, the sleeper had to be a man. And a heavyset one, at that, probably with globs of pale flesh bulging out of his pajamas.

And then there was the gut-wrenching smell. Nauseating. It was high time to leave.

I eased the door shut. Turned around.

A figure of someone standing in the moonlight, a ghostly sentinel. Staring at me.

My throat filled up with a silent scream.

"You finally came," she said.

"Damn it!" I hissed, my heart hammering inside.

"I gave up on you. Thought you'd quit on me." She spoke loudly, as if she were in broad daylight walking down Main Street on a Sunday afternoon.

"Did you have to spook me like that?"

"I was here the whole time. You're blind as a bat." Her tone was berating.

"Shh! Someone's sleeping in there." I pointed with my finger.

She shook her head. "Don't worry about him. He could sleep through an earthquake."

"Is that your dad?"

She nodded, a certain fear in her eyes.

I stepped off the porch, away from the stench of the house, stumbled out to the middle of the yard, and lifted my face to the moonlight with all the relish of a pale sunbather on the first warm day of summer. The air out there, which only five minutes ago seemed disgusting, I now found as fresh and crisp as Denver mountain air.

"What the hell am I doing here?" I whispered. "What is it that you wanted to show me?"

"Didn't say I wanted to show you anything."

"You did. You wrote that you had something to show me."

"No. I said I have something to *tell* you."

I looked at her. In the pale moonlight, she stood like a scarecrow in a field of discarded detritus, snipped of strength and muscle tone, a sallow stick figure. Only her lips had color. As she walked over to me, I noticed, to my horror, that she was wearing some bright red lipstick. But she'd overstepped the parameters of her lips and given them a bloated, swollen look as if she'd just been sucker-punched on the mouth. She wanted to look pretty for me.

"Look at this place," I said. "How can you live here?"

"It ain't half bad," she said. "I already cleaned it up some 'fore you got here."

"You're kidding, right?" Piles of trash lay strewn about, no doubt home to all kinds of varmints and ticks. The air was redolent with decomposition.

"Why did you ask me to come here?" I asked.

"You're the one with the bike," she explained. "I ain't walkin' if I don't have to."

"But why not at school? Why—?"

"Because you ignore me at school. As if I ain't even there. Won't even look at me."

"That's because we have nothing to talk about."

"We have what we know."

"What are you talking about?"

"You don't need to be so uptight about it. You know," she said, looking directly at me. Her eyes dropped down, pausing fleetingly at my lips before falling away to the ground. "That."

I diverted my eyes downwards. "I still don't know what you're talking about," I mumbled.

She looked at me incredulously. "You know exactly what I'm talking about. Our secret."

I shuffled my feet. "Yeah, well, what about it?"

She smiled to herself and waggled her eyebrows at me. "Why don't we sit down a little?" she suggested. "So we can talk." A flirtatious smirk embroidered itself onto her lips.

"Listen to me," I said. "Just tell me what you know."

"And I will. But let's sit first." She reached for my arm as if to lead me.

"Tell me now!" I hissed at her, slashing my arm away. "You drag me out here in the middle of the night, and all you want to do is just *tell* me something?" I brushed at the sleeve where her hand had briefly touched. "Tell me now, or I'm leaving! I have no time for your games."

"Why don't we sit? Why don't we, like, do what we did on the stage? Why don't we just sit?" Her face contorted into a plea. Then her hand clutched my coat sleeve; she suddenly flopped down, pulling me down with her.

We landed hard on some planks of rotten wood. My left elbow took the brunt of the fall; a jolt of electricity shot up my arm.

She continued to speak, hurriedly, as if she knew she only had a few seconds before I collected myself. "I thought we could continue what we started. I thought we stopped when we could have, you know, continued and stuff." She edged herself closer to me.

And despite myself, I felt my heart begin to tremor. I hated myself for feeling this way, but no girl had ever liked me before in my life. Ever. I tried to stay angry with Jan, but a different kind of passion began to arouse itself in me. There was a little careless freckle in the soft indent of her neck. Inexplicably, I suddenly found myself wanting to kiss it.

She placed her hand on mine; I pulled my hand away. "Stop it," I hissed. "Just stop it."

A geyser of hurt exploded in her eyes. She shrank from me, retreating back into the light. A world of rejection was in her wobbling lips.

Then, feline-like, she pounced on me. At first I thought she was attacking me, and I tried to find her wrists to thwart her from clawing me. She landed on top of me, pushing me down onto my back. It was then I understood her true intent. Her lips, rimmed with hard determination, found mine. And with her lipstick on, it was like kissing a greasy, cold keyboard. She made absurd smacking noises. I felt her oily, pimpled forehead against mine, as greasy as her overly rouged lips.

"Stop it!" I yelled. "Get off me *now!*"

And just like that, she froze.

Slowly she rose and backed off, growing smaller in the darkness. Diminishing. I panted hard, panicked. Brushing my legs and arms, I picked myself up.

"Don't you like me?" she asked me. Her voice came out kind of spry. "When we kissed, I thought—I mean, the way you kissed me back, I thought you liked me. I thought that was our secret."

I cringed. I thought to tell her the truth, to tell her that there was nothing in her personality that enthralled me, nor much in her looks either. That when I had kissed her back, I'd simply been caught up in the throes of something that had taken me by complete surprise. That when I pictured the image of the two of us walking around the school hallways hand-in-hand or sitting at the movie theater together, all I could see was one word: *ludicrous.*

I turned on my heel and started walking. "I'm leaving."

I'd gotten no more than ten paces when she said, "Why don't you give me a chance?"

I kept on walking to my bike.

"All I want is to get out of this hellhole. Do you think I like it? Do you think I like being hated by everyone?"

I turned around. "Look, I'm leaving."

"I'm just like you, you know."

"You're *nothing* like me," I spat.

She nodded. "You and me, we're just the same. Nobody pays attention to us. People take one look at us and dismiss us. Like nothing. Like we're nothing."

"Speak for yourself."

"You're a loner, Kris."

"Like I said: speak for yourself. I've got friends. I've got Naomi."

"And I've got my dad. I tell him everything. He knows everything that goes on. He knows all the kids I hate at school. He knows about you. So he's a little wrecked in his head, especially without his medication, but I've got him. So you've got Naomi. So what? We're still nobodies."

"Like. I. Said. Speak. For. Yourself. Am. I. Speaking. Slowly. Enough. For. You?"

"I left a gift for you today," she said, her voice pleading. "I left it for you in your backpack."

Her declaration, so simple and direct, caught me off guard. "The knife?" I hissed. "You're the one who put the knife in my bag?"

"Calm down. I did it as a gift. For you. Something you really need. You told me how you were chased the other day, so I thought you should carry this. For your protection."

"Do you know how stupid...don't you know the trouble you've gotten me into because—?"

"It's the only thing I could think of!" she shouted back. "I don't have money, and it was lying in the kitchen, so I took it, OK? When my dad wasn't looking. And gave it to you. I thought you'd like it."

I flung my arms into the air, my insides burning.

"Look, I'm sorry, OK? I just meant well. I thought you'd like it."

I turned and began storming away.

"Where are you going?" she asked.

"Don't ever give me anything again. Don't ever even talk to me again. Don't even think about me. Don't *anything* me."

"Please, Kris," she implored, "stay for a bit. Don't go. I won't do nothin'. We don't have to kiss or nothin', you know, we can just, like, be here together. It doesn't—"

I ignored her and strode faster towards my bike.

"Kris!" she shouted after me.

I turned; her face was lit by the silvery moonlight, the squalor of her home strewn around her. Then the light subsided: she dissolved into her surroundings. And she spoke with a wavering voice that a convict might use when pleading with the executioner. "I think I like you."

"Well, that's obvious," I said contemptuously.

She flinched a little at that. "No. No," she said, shaking her head from side to side. "It's just that I..." Her fingers wrangled one another as she spoke. "I care for you, Kris. I really, really want to be with you. I see something in you that others don't. Even on that first day in class when I looked at you, I knew. That you're special and...and...I care for you a lot. I think I even lo—"

"No!"

"I said that I—"

"Are you crazy?"

"No, I—"

"You don't even know me!"

And then it hit me. In choosing to kiss me—out of all the other guys in school—she was basically picking the one person she had the best chance with. She looked to the very bottom of the totem pole of born-losers at school and saw me. The Chinese kid with badly matching clothes and a dorky haircut. In my mind, I spat on her.

"I do know you, Kris," she said meekly. "Don't you like me even a little?"

"Why would I like you? What's there to like about you?"

Her face didn't register any surprise or shock. She took it in, deadpan. "Why did you kiss me back, then?" she asked with quiet resignation.

I acted as if I hadn't heard her. "You're fugly. You're stupid," I went on. I was relentless. "I don't know what I'm doing here with you. Don't ever talk to me again, you stupid slut."

I had never said such words to anyone before, nor even imagined the possibility of it. But I've learned a few things about life since then, and one of them is that everyone must have someone to feel superior to. It is a necessity of life. Even bottom-dwellers must find a roach to step on.

She stepped back, aghast. I sensed something inside her reeling backwards. I should have felt shame, but instead I found release, a purging of that embarrassing kissing incident I'd had with her.

Then a meanness in her eyes suddenly lashed at me, wet and glinting. "But I do know you, Kris. Better than you think!" she said with surprising force. "Better than you might possibly think!"

"You know nothing about me!"

"You're just like everyone else," she retorted. "You're just as bad as them—"

"Shut up!" I yelled.

"I thought you were different from the rest—"

"I *am* different," I spat back at her, my voice filled with venom. "Just look at me—look at my hair, look at my eyes, look at my face. I *am* different."

We glared at each other.

"I take back what I said," she said, her chest heaving up and down.

"What?"

"I take it all back. Everything. Everything I said to you."

I backpedaled two or three steps, turned, and began to walk away.

"Kris!" she shouted, her voice hotly urgent.

I hated it when she said my name; it implied a level of intimacy we didn't share. I thought she was going to rail on about something or follow me, but she didn't say another word. By the time I turned the bike around and hoisted myself onto the seat, she had vanished. When I twisted around one last time before careening around a bend, my bike dangerously wavering, I saw nothing but a vacant clearing in front of her home blighted in the tombstone-gray light of the crescent moon.

THE NEW YORK TIMES

DECEMBER 19

Into an ever-deepening mystery that has tormented the town of Ashland comes further tragedy: yet another Slackenkill High School student has mysteriously disappeared.

The circumstances surrounding this particular disappearance are even more harrowing due to the level of violence so evidently—and some would say tauntingly—displayed. Police were led by teachers to a girls' bathroom in the east wing of the school early yesterday where freshman Trey Logan's severed right hand was discovered in a trashcan.

Shock and panic spread quickly through the hallways and classrooms of the school just as morning classes were beginning. In the mayhem and bedlam that ensued, local city police failed to effectively cordon off the area and may have lost valuable evidence—if not suspects—from right under their noses.

Officials, who confirmed late yesterday afternoon that fingerprints taken from the hand were indeed Mr. Logan's, have been quick to

add that they are still holding out hope
for the victim. He was last seen yesterday
evening at a local bowling alley with some
friends. He was wearing a green North Face
jacket, Gap blue jeans, and brown boots—ge-
neric fare, acknowledged the police spokes-
person, but he added that Mr. Logan regularly
wore a very distinctive gold chain around his
neck with his initials emblazoned on it. Anyone with any information is urged to contact
the police hotline number immediately. The
FBI, which has admitted to clandestine in-
vestigations over the past few weeks, had no
comment to make except that they were working
"in conjunction with local law enforcement,"
doing everything they could. They added that
the latest disappearance, while tragic, might
nevertheless help officials solve the serial abductions by clues perhaps inadvertently
left behind.

DECEMBER 19

Fresh mozzarella with prosciutto, tomatoes, and basil oil. Minestrone soup with a sprinkling of basil leaves. Lasagna layered with meat ragu, béchamel, and roasted garlic. And to top it all off, a decadent hot fudge sundae.

"That was pretty fantastic," I said to Miss Durgenhoff. She was sitting at the end of the bed, an apron tied around her waist. "I've never had dinner in bed."

"Well, when I saw you come home, you looked beat," she said cheerily. "Figured you crashed on your bed when you didn't come down for the longest. So...well, voila."

"You're definitely spoiling me."

"Consider it a thank you. For all the ways you've been kind to me."

"Hardly."

"And as extra fuel for the coming few days. With the musical and all, you'll need it. It's so close now—just a few more days."

I shook my head in disbelief. "Four more days. Hard to imagine."

She smiled whimsically. "You'll be fine. Great, in fact."

"Next two days are crucial. Mr. Matthewman hates the fact that I still haven't practiced with the chorus yet. So we have rehearsals with the chorus, dress rehearsals with the orchestra, he whole works, from morning to night. He's really packed it in."

"Well, it couldn't be helped, right? You were an eleventh-hour replacement. And there were exigent circumstances."

"I suppose. Anyway, the next couple of days are key. Pretty nervous, I have to tell you."

She smiled at me with those winsome eyes of hers. For a few moments we sat in an easy silence.

"It's actually me who has to thank you, Miss Durgenhoff."

"Oh? How so?"

"Well, I don't know."

Miss Durgenhoff laughed a little. "That's OK." She smiled wider. "You don't have to say anything."

I propped myself up higher. "No, I should. You encouraged me. About my singing."

"Oh, it was nothing. Hard not to praise natural talent, after all. You're going to be great. Amazing."

I tugged on my blanket. "Sometimes I don't know if I've really got it in me," I said after a while. "It still feels so unreal to me. I keep imagining the worst that could happen. Like catching a cold or something, and my voice just goes kaput overnight."

Miss Durgenhoff smoothed the front of her apron. "I seriously doubt that's going to happen," she said. "I've been hearing you sing, and you have such a commanding voice, strong. A voice with some real backbone and muscle. I don't see it petering out."

"I hope not." I took another scoop of the sundae. "Mr. Matthewman says I emotionally check out of my songs way too much. He wants me to find passion every time." I stared down at my plate, shaking my head slightly. "I don't know how to do that. Like, how can you be passionate *every* time?"

"Oh, that you most certainly can do," she said. The sudden seriousness in her tone surprised me.

"How's that?"

"You just need to plug into yourself more. Find that thing in you which *moves* you. For some, it's fear; for others, it's love. But just tap into that, and you'll inject passion into your singing."

I shrugged my shoulders. "I don't think I have that. I'm just an ordinary guy, nothing deep down."

She snapped up her head and gave me a strange look. "Mind if I go on a mild spiel for a bit?" she asked.

"Sure," I said warily.

"Something about you has always concerned me. It's not obvious, it's below the surface, but..." She smoothed her apron again. "But there's anger in you. Huge amounts. Behind all your timidity, there's something really teeming deep inside. I can't quite pin it down, but you're like this plush, well-made bed with something hidden underneath. Withdrawn, quiet on the outside, but inside...it's quite unsettling sometimes."

"Yeah, like that secret painting thing of yours," I laughed, but then I stopped. She was being serious.

"Just saying that if you really want to sing with passion, just tap into that." She looked like she wanted to say more, but then she stopped, shaking her head. "OK, that was weird," she said, *tsk tsking* herself. "Don't know what got a hold of me."

"No, it's OK. Thanks for dinner."

"No need to thank me, Kris," she said gently, smiling. She stood up, lifting the tray off my lap. Her kneecaps popped a little, and she tittered to herself. "Sitting too long again, I'm afraid." She walked to the door, favoring her right leg as she hobbled away, then she turned back and smiled reassuringly. "You'll be wonderful." She turned to leave.

"Miss Durgenhoff?"

"Yes?"

"If you're free, it'd be great if you could come to the performance. I have a few seats allotted to me—choice seats, mind you."

"The perks of being a lead," she said with a grin.

"Can you come? It'll be great to have you there."

"I'd love to. It would be nice to see you with a full orchestral accompaniment. In your costume and all that."

I nodded quickly. "I'll get you a ticket."

She smiled at that. "That's very thoughtful. But truthfully, I'll have to see how my legs hold up. Weather's doing them no favors, let me tell you. But thank you." She winked at me as she hobbled out.

The room seemed very empty and very quiet after that. I thought to get out of bed and maybe help her with the dishes, but I soon found myself drowsy again. I drifted off to sleep.

Bad things always seem to happen in the middle of the night.

Miss Durgenhoff shook me awake. "It's your mother" was all she said.

We drove to the hospital where my mother worked. The roads were deserted that time of night, as if holding a respectful silence. Miss Durgenhoff—driving as fast as she dared—told me what they'd told her on the phone. My mother had been carting away some laundry and collapsed. She'd lost consciousness.

My mother was sedated when we walked into her room, lit only by a dim, beeping monitor. Even with her eyes closed, her face was wrought with strain. "A very minor stroke," the doctor informed us in a quiet voice. "The CAT scan shows no significant damage. She'll make a full recovery." He stared down at his notepad. "Staff here said she's seemed tired of late. The stroke was probably brought on by physical and mental exhaustion. She needs her rest and..." I stopped listening.

They let me stay. Even after the sedation ran its course, she slept without stirring for twenty-four hours. I sat by her the whole time, melding my body into the unyielding corners of the plastic chair. It was mostly quiet. Occasionally the other patient in the room, a fragile woman as wrinkled as the bedsheets she tousled, would cry out with frightened, irrational words. But she'd always quickly fall back to sleep.

Mr. Matthewman was understanding on the phone. "Musical, schmusical," he said. He told me to stay with my mother, to not worry about the rehearsals. "I'll keep the dogs at bay," he said. But I could sense uncertainty in his voice.

It was on the second night, while I was sitting half-asleep next to her, that my mother finally came to.

"He always wanted to come to America," she suddenly said as if in mid-conversation, her voice surprisingly clear and strong in the opaque dark. "Even on our first date, chatting in the teahouse, he spoke of it. America. America. America. It was his dream. You should have seen him back then, the way his eyes would shine, the way he'd talk so excitedly, spit would fly out." She stared at the ceiling, her eyes moist.

"It was all he talked about," she continued. "America. I bought into it, eventually, of course. That kind of passion, it's contagious, especially to an adoring wife. And on the day you were born, Xing, he made me two promises. First, he promised he would do everything humanly possible to take care of his family. And then, his second promise: he would bring us to America. Right there in the delivery room, you not even an hour old, he bent down and looked me in the eye and promised me. He was so serious, I laughed, tired as I was." She smiled faintly, lost in the memories.

"It did not seem possible...it did not seem right that he would die here, and so soon." She paused for a long time, as if catching her breath. "With him gone, I realized something I always knew deep down but never admitted: America was never my dream. It was never something I wanted for myself. And I realized how much I hated being here. America." She spat out the last word. Her eyes fell down and met mine for just a moment, then they flicked back up as if she were repulsed. "He would never have thought that after so many years...this would be all we have to show for it."

"It's not so bad," I lied.

She fell quiet as if done in. A line of tears fell from the corners of her eyelids, streaking down to her pillow. She thought I did not understand the level of her shame. She thought I did not know what she did at the massage parlor during the day. The men who came, the places she touched. She believed she held a secret too bitter, too shameful for me to ever know. But I did know.

"Why didn't we go back to China after Father died?" I asked. "Why have we stayed here?"

Her voice, when it came, was sharp. "Do you remember the night we left China? When we swam to the ship?" She went on, not seeing my head nodding. "That night, once safely aboard, he made me promise. Made me. That we would never leave America. Ever." She shook her head. "Maybe he sensed some hesitancy in me, even back then. He was so persistent. Gripped my hands until I promised." She dried her tears with her wrist.

She was exhausted. I saw it in her motionless body, dead weight on gray bedsheets, weariness pressing upon her face. She would drift off now; I sensed that. She would retreat into her shell, the same way she had cocooned herself from me after his death.

"We should have gone back to China," I said. "It would have been better for us."

After a long moment, her mouth opened and she spoke words I have never forgotten.

"Your father believed you had a gift."

I stared at her.

"And that America would give you the best chance to develop it," she said. "I think that's what made him so determined to stay here, mostly anyway. For your gift."

"What gift?" I asked, my heart suddenly beating hard.

She turned to look at me, surprise on her face. "Have you forgotten so quickly, Xing?" She shook her head slowly. "You once could really sing. You once had an amazing voice." A sadness entered her eyes, but there was a hint of anger in her voice. "Your father thought puberty robbed you of your voice. But it wasn't puberty, was it? It was America."

I sat stunned. My father had never told me this. There were times when I had sensed his encouragement for me to sing and, in the latter years, his disappointment when I refused to. But I did not know my father had believed in me so. And this knowledge nearly overwhelmed me.

"I guess I have something to tell you," I whispered.

When she didn't respond, I told her. As simply as I could, my voice trembling at times with excitement, and with not a little fear. I could still sing. I had won the lead in the school musical. That the musical was in two nights, and I wanted her to be there.

For an agonizing, drawn-out moment, she did not say anything. Her face remained passive, unresponsive. "You said it was the lead?" she asked at last.

"Yes. It's the lead. I have five solos. They're beautiful songs, and my voice is getting better every day. My voice coach is terrific. I can really sing again."

She nodded, then closed her eyes, pulling the blanket over her chest. She nodded again, softer this time, approvingly. "That is good," she said. "Your father would be proud." And then she gave in to fatigue. Sleep consumed her within seconds.

I did not sleep that night. I sat all night, my mind racing, my heart pounding. Something like hope stirred in me; something like joy kept me awake.

I sang softly to myself, my songs, until the dawn sun trimmed the dark drapes with light.

DECEMBER 22

I breathed in.

And when I exhaled, I felt the surge of my lungs, the power flowing out of them. I angled my larynx to bring out the desired sounds, tweaked miniscule muscles for the most dramatic of tonal fluctuations. I had total mastery of the sounds I sang: the pitch, the depth, the tonal base, the melodious warbles. I knew how to split nuances into vast ranges of feeling. There was a marked difference in my singing.

Mr. Matthewman, my audience of one that morning, was ecstatic. "I don't know what you did at the hospital over the past two days, kid, but it's brilliant." He looked at me, every feature of his face seemingly accented with an exclamation mark. "Brilliant!"

I nodded. It *was* brilliant.

"Well," he said, getting up from his piano and stool and walking over to me. "You've arrived, Kris. At the perfect moment, too. Not a day too soon." He placed his hands on my shoulders. "Tonight, at the dress rehearsal, you're going to shine. You're going to shock the world," he gushed. Then he sighed heavily. "Never," he said, excitedly shaking his head from side to side, "never would I ever have wanted to wait so long to give you a chance to practice with the chorus. To sing before the teachers. But there were unforeseen, unfortunate circumstances…" He looked down at me. "Your mother doing all right then?"

I nodded. "Should be returning home later this morning. She's promised to come to the show. She's excited."

He patted me hard on the shoulders again, almost thumping down on me. "You'll show them, kid. You'll show them all."

"I'll show them," I said.

"That's the spirit!" he added. He went to his piano and rummaged through some paper. "I thought I put it in here somewhere…" he muttered to himself. "Aha!" he said, bringing out a piece of paper. "You need to go to room five twenty-four at lunchtime today. Miss Jenkins will be there to give you your costume. She worked in overdrive mode over the weekend to finish it. Said she scrapped her original once she realized her work was probably going to be photographed and taped by the media."

"Five twenty-four. Lunchtime. I'll be there."

"And be nice, Kris. You know what she can be like." He rolled his eyes.

"Who? The dragon lady?"

He chuckled. "Now, before you go, some last words of advice. No hollering or screaming, no excessive talking, OK? We really need to protect your voice. OK? Basically, you really should keep to yourself today and tomorrow."

That, I thought, would not be a problem.

"Stay out of the cold—it'll shred your voice to tatters if you don't watch out. A long, hot bath tonight after the rehearsal. Soak in it for at least an hour. Plenty of sleep. Try to get at least nine hours tonight, if not more. What else am I forgetting? Oh, yes—an afternoon nap tomorrow if you can.

Come in here, catch a few Zs at around four or five. You can sleep on the couch. Eat something before five but not after—it'll pay hellfire to your butterflies if you do, and it might make you drowsy."

"Mr. Matthewman?"

"Yes? What is it?"

"I was wondering about the tickets..."

He smacked his forehead. "But of course." He fished into his inner pocket and took out ten tickets. "As promised. Your wish is my command," he said in his best genie voice. "Do you know how expensive those tickets have become?" He shook his head. "With all the media coverage, this school's making a windfall."

"I'll only be needing three tickets."

"Three? But you've been allotted ten. You're the lead, after all, Kris."

"Even so, three's enough for me."

"Here, take all ten." He handed me the tickets. "Sell the extras on eBay—you'll make a killing." He winked at me. "You didn't hear it from me, of course, right?"

"Who are you bringing?" I thought this was a safe way to ask about his personal life. He never alluded to any family or friends. He was guarded about his past.

"Oh, I have some old colleagues of mine driving up from the city. It's a big event, this one."

"Old friends?"

"I'm not sure I'd call them friends," he said, raking back hair from his eyes. "Just people I knew when I was at Julliard."

I packed my bag and zipped it up. Then something occurred to me.

"When we meet again tomorrow morning...will that be our last practice?"

The question caught him a little off guard. "Huh. I haven't really thought about it. Well, I suppose it would be." He shook his head. "But we can't let things like that distract us right now. Tomorrow night, Kris. The big night is tomorrow night. Stay focused on that."

"And there's no chance of any last-minute cancellation?"

"What are you talking about? Of the performance?" He saw me nod at him. "Of course not."

"It's just that I thought...maybe Mr. Marsworth is facing a lot of public pressure to cancel the show. I can see him folding if he senses that public sentiment leaning that way."

"There's nothing to worry about, Kris," he said. "In the end, everything will come together. You'll see."

"How can you be so sure? I mean, there's no telling what might happen. There might even be another disappearance. Who knows when the guy might strike again? He's been anything but predictable, after all."

"No, that's not going to happen."

"How can you be so sure?"

"I give you my assurance, Kris." His voice was firm as he spoke; he stood up and walked over to me, placing his hand on the back of my neck. It was warm and sweaty, and I flinched at the touch.

"The show will go on." There was a flinty glint in his eye. "I guarantee you this." And his hand grew hot on my skin as if suddenly charged. His fingers twitched on the nape of my neck, energized by some sudden prospect. He shook his head as if clearing it. "Well, off you go," he said.

I grabbed my backpack, nodded a quick good-bye, and left. The door closed with a thud behind me. And right outside the classroom, taped on the wall, was a *Missing* poster. The faces on the poster jumped out at me: Anthony Hasbourd. Winston Barnes. Trey Logan. Their smiles were accusatory, and their eyes, even through the black and white photocopy, were snappish and castigating.

I wondered where they were at that very moment. Imprisoned somewhere far away, in the dark basement of some weirdo, the unwilling participants to his psychosis? Or lying facedown in the woods somewhere, or face up drifting down the river, or stuffed into a refrigerator and dumped at a landfill? I stared at the three of them, trying to find some resemblance, some common trait that might have drawn the abductor to them in the first place. But where one was wimpy, another was filled with brawn. Where one lacked intelligence, another was filled with academic potential. Nothing seemed to tie the three together. Except their eyes, of course. With a singular feeling, they glared at me. I hated the way they looked. They seemed to know something I didn't.

DECEMBER 22, DRESS REHEARSAL

I t was night, and the shepherds sat upon the fields. Sheep of varying sizes grazed under the pitted sky, their forms as stationary as the stars above. The shepherds rested easy, their calloused hands laid soft against the smooth bark of their rod and staff. A slight breeze blew across the land, drawing with it the musty smell of wet weeds and the dank odor of toil and sweat. It was a night like countless thousands.

Then the heads of the sheep suddenly lifted in unison, their noses pointed up and towards the northern mountains, their bodies stiffening ever so slightly. Under their hooded attire, the shepherds barely moved, but their eyes were alert now, their fingertips edging around the curves of their staffs. It was an angel. It started to float towards them, its arms raised in consoling fashion, its face a picture of chaste radiance, white wings sprouting from behind. It glided closer and closer, sailing across the terrain...then it tripped over its feet.

The speakers screeched with feedback. A stagehand turned the auditorium lights on.

"Oh, Samantha, I thought I told you to be careful about the wires. If you can't remember to step over them in rehearsal, there's no way you're going to remember tomorrow night."

"Sorry, Miss Jenkins," Samantha said, picking herself up. As she patted down the front of her costume, a little plume of dust mushroomed out.

"Oh," sighed Miss Jenkins tragically, "the wing is all bent out of shape now. Come here, let me fix it."

The real world broke in. The glaring spotlights, the impatient, demanding teachers sipping from coffee cups. Wired models of sheep standing at bay, disheveled cotton wool shed on the floor beneath. The lingering smell of glue in the air, of varnish and fresh paint. Around me, tired students shifted in their costumes, weary from a dress rehearsal gone awry. After two hours of practice, we'd gotten only ten minutes into the show; I'd yet to sing even a note.

A five-minute break was called. A number of students made their way to the bathroom. Police officers, pulling some serious overtime, sauntered over to the connecting hallway. I stayed behind, finding a seat on the front row.

"Kris." It was Miss Jenkins standing in front of me.

"Yes?"

"I trust you're ready to sing?"

I nodded my head. "I'm ready."

"Well, Theodore has told me good things about you."

I smiled awkwardly, not knowing what to say.

"What we're going to do," she said, tapping her clipboard, "is skip a few scenes so we can squeeze you in tonight. Get in at least a few of your songs. I think it's important that we get to hear you," she said, her voice stilted.

"Thank you."

"You're welcome," she said pertly, and she walked away.

The students wandered back slowly, looking tired. Miss Jenkins lifted her spindly finger into the air and announced that practice would resume.

Except practice never did resume. I was standing in the middle of the stage all alone, readying myself for the solo. The stage had been set. The orchestral music had already begun. I sensed all eyes zeroed in on me, curious, expectant. I breathed in and felt a pocket of air gather in my lungs. *Let it germinate in there*, I could hear Mr. Matthewman's gravelly voice saying. *Let it crystallize into sweet musical notes.*

It was only then as the lights dimmed down that I first noticed the swiveling blue, red, and white lights sashaying on the ceiling. We all blinked at those lights, none of us, I don't think, really understanding their true import at the time. But then gazes shifted away from the ceiling and towards the high windows. The siren lights radiated in like a sickly rainbow.

And then suddenly the door to the auditorium opened. A voice yelled out, heard clearly even above the dying, discordant notes of the orchestra. "They've found the bodies! They've found the bodies! In the pond, they've found the bodies!"

All thoughts of the show ground to a halt. The air in my lungs halted mid-flight, plummeted to the ground.

There was a pictorial beauty about the next few moments, a slavish energy to them that seemed to emblazon punctuated images into my memory. I remember them with both an ease and a revulsion: the ease with which one recalls the most whimsical of memories, the revulsion of nightmarish images that won't go away.

In my memory, silence pervades the whole scene. This cannot be; surely there must have been shouts, screams, worried cries, the crackle of police radios filling the air. But in my memory there is only silence, the silence of a mime where the whole troupe of actors move in a seamless, effortless synchronization with one another. If there was a cry of protest from Miss Jenkins, we didn't hear it, nor do I hear it in my memory. We scampered down the scaffolding; we rushed down the auditorium steps; we jumped out of the orchestra pit; yet there was no sharpness to our movements, no herky-jerky. It was all an aqueous slide, a silky flow out of the auditorium, a stream of light mercury pouring out.

And then we were running, gliding along the fields toward the pond. The siren lights from afar splashed languidly on the ground before us, soft, lazy sweeps of blue then red then white. We must have run for a minute, at least, but in my mind there is no effort, no exertion in our legs or chests. There is only the softened glee of children flying to the circus as one.

Even when we reached the pond, even when we saw that they were pulling the sodden bodies out of the break in the ice, the reverie continued. There must have been police officers intercepting us, for I can see them in my mind holding outstretched arms towards us. But they look more like ringmasters beckoning us to come closer, to take a closer look. And there were yellow ticker tapes on the perimeter, but in the matte-dulled lights of revolving red, white, and blue, they look drained of color, indecisive. Off to the side was a man in a jogging suit, hugging himself, his dog rapt at the end of a taut leash, still barking, its breath gusting out of its mouth in thick, loutish clouds ...

Two bodies are lying on the ground, shining with wetness. The ice water has preserved them—Anthony Hasbourd and Winston Barnes, pale white as stripped mannequins. A peaceful expression on their faces, as if they have only just fallen asleep while gazing up at the canopy of stars above. And the last body is now being pulled out, stiff and unwieldy, and laid on the icy ground. Trey Logan. And just before a blanket is hastily drawn over him, I see his open eyes, pools of black set in harsh relief against the shock of whiteness that covers his face. The eyes stare at me with pinpointed condemnation.

Even an hour after the bodies were discovered, police kept pouring into school, carpeting the fields with swiveling siren lights. Reporters rushed over, their cars and vans careening around the slick roads. Uniformed officers began dispersing the swelling crowds, but I was already gone by then.

I biked to church. Not to seek some kind of spiritual solace, but because Naomi was there. At some kind of youth group meeting where she'd be singing on the worship team or sitting in a circle studying the Bible. I needed someone to talk to. I needed Naomi.

It was so dark and quiet in the sanctuary at first that I thought everyone had already left. But then I heard a murmuring of voices coming from a corner in the front. There was a group of them, hunched over, praying. I sat down in the back pew, far removed, and waited. My back was slick with perspiration. I waited.

There were only a few of them tonight, no more than ten. Attendance was sparse, affected no doubt by the disappearances. There were long periods of silence interspersed with short, somber prayers. I saw Naomi sitting on the steps leading to the pulpit. A faint haze of light fell on her; her head hung down against a kneecap, and she barely moved. Her slim porcelain arms extended out of her sleeveless turtleneck like white silk. I looked away.

Not too long after, they finished with a chorus of soft amens. I stood up; Naomi saw me immediately and came over.

"What are *you* doing here?" she said, surprised.

"Hey, just wanted to see how you are."

"You're all hot and sweaty. Did you bike here?"

I nodded, then began to tell her about the discovery of the bodies at the pond. Her eyes widened as I spoke, her hand clasping me tightly on the arm.

"Jason should know," she said as she spun around, referring to the pastor's son. "Come on, let's tell him."

"Wait, Naomi." I touched her on the shoulder.

She paused and looked at me. "What is it?"

"I need to tell you something," I said urgently. I glanced around. A few of her church friends were observing us from the front, not openly, but with curious, sideway glances. "Not here, OK? I can't do it here with all these people around." Maybe it was the bodies I'd just seen, how tangible they made the possibility of death, but I found that I could no longer wait. Enough pussyfooting around. I looked at her. "There's something I've been meaning to tell you for a long time."

And then the most amazing thing happened. Her eyes suddenly softened like diamonds melting, glistening with a new wetness.

"Look," she said, and stepped a little closer to me. "I've wanted to talk to you, too. We've both been so busy, it's been forever since we've had a chance just to talk." She reached out and took my hand. I could smell her shampoo, she was so close to me. "During the time we've barely seen each other, something amazing happened." She was smiling now and stepped even closer. "I've come to realize something."

The light was hitting her eyes just right, illuminating their deepest pools. I could see beautiful brown flecks in her eyes.

Barely able to speak, I whispered, "I know. I've realized something, too."

Her eyes widened, then moistened even more. Her hand touching mine was soft, gentle; it was Naomi holding my hand in a way she never had. Fifty moonlight kisses were nothing compared to that one touch on my arm.

"Naomi," I whispered. "I feel the same way. I know. I know."

Her eyes flashed with surprise. "I didn't know you knew."

"How long have we known each other, Naomi?" I asked her tenderly. "I know you better than anyone else does."

And just then, the moment was destroyed. A couple of teen boys moved into our space, clearly wanting to speak with Naomi. I backed off.

"Let's talk later, OK, Xing?" she said crisply, cleanly.

As I watched her, I realized I had underestimated Naomi's rise to superstardom in the church. She had gone from pew-warmer to attention-getter to godly princess. There'd been hints of this meteoric rise, but the days of suggestion were now officially over. Now the boys were going to start moving in on her like a tsunami wave. On Sundays at church, in her frilly summer dress, or at picnics in her spaghetti-stringed shirts and short-shorts, they were going to swarm her. Like they were already beginning to do now.

Afterwards, she came to me, glowing from all the attention.

"Whew," she said, feigning exhaustion. "Too many people." She made a show of arching her eyebrows in fatigue.

"Do you have some time we can talk now?" I asked her. I sat close to her, the length of our arms almost touching.

"I think so. Until the next batch of people comes running for my advice."

I paused, not really sure how to proceed.

"Jason told me the police are all over school," she said.

"Yeah, they got there pretty quickly."

"He also heard that they really botched it. They didn't seal the area off quickly enough. Again."

I nodded, remembering the crowds of people. "Onlookers got there pretty fast. Everybody's curious, everybody's afraid." I shook my head. "We had to cancel rehearsal."

"Aw, that's too bad. But you'll be ready for tomorrow night, right?" She smiled at no one in particular. "But, wow, it gets me every time. I still can't believe you're the lead." She saw my reaction. "No, I mean that in a good way," she said, placing her hand for a fleeting moment on my arm. "So, big Broadway star, how does it feel to be just a day away from your debut?"

"I guess it's OK."

"Whatever," she said, grinning. "Whatever you say, Mr. Man of Jerusalem. Not to sound corny, but you are The Man."

I shook my head. "There're more important things going on." I turned to look at her. "What's going on with you," I continued quickly, "that's more important."

She stared at me for a moment, slightly bemused. Then she broke into a smile. "Oh, Xing, that's so sweet." Then she patted my shoulder.

She *patted* my shoulder. As one would a cute puppy.

I sat very still, sensing something off-kilter about this moment.

"I just can't understand," she went on, "how you found out about us. We've been careful to keep it a secret."

I did not say anything. A sodden, cold weight hit me on the back of my head. I fought against it. I straightened my back and lifted my chin.

"Oh," she said, gushing, "here he comes."

Of course, it was a white boy; of course, it was the pastor's son. Of course, he was attractive with sparkling blue eyes. Of course, he had a good build, was sensitive and spiritual, and of course, he was a great guy.

She cuddled up next to him. He was taller than me, broader than me, handsomer than me, spoke English better than me.

"Jason, this is Kris."

And of course, his grip was firmer than mine.

"Kris, great to meet you. Nai's told me all about you."

It was awkward for about three seconds. But I could be strong before her. I could fight off the waves of disappointment. The next words out of my mouth were, "Tell me how you met, please."

Naomi jumped at the opportunity, her words spilling out in joyful abandon.

I didn't hear a word she said. Something about church, something about chemistry, something about the same wavelength. If she said more, I missed it. I blanked out on her words. I felt only one emotion. Betrayal. I wanted to grab her by the throat and ask how she could do this, how she could betray me by going out with one of them. I wanted to punch her; I wanted to kiss her.

I was afraid, too, but I shoved the fear aside. Back then, I didn't know what I was afraid of, but now I do. I was afraid of the great well of loneliness that awaited me.

I felt her slipping away, even as she spoke. And after a while, she did slip away, with him, the white boyfriend. I could tell that they wanted to hold hands; perhaps once outside, alone in the car, they did. It was all I could take.

★

I biked to the mall, thinking of nothing. It was cold. I bought a movie ticket, walked into the closest theater, and to this day cannot recall a single image. When I came out I was hungry, and it was dark, and I had no money for food.

It was a long ride back, and I was freezing by the time I got home.

I sat on my bed with the lights off. I was numb; numb from the cold, numb from shock, numb from betrayal. It did not matter to me that I was shivering on the bed. It did not matter to me that the house was draped in complete darkness, bereft of a single sound within.

Moonlight angled into my room in refracted beams. Everything in the room was burnished into the mercuric colors of black and white. Everything, that is, except for the painting bursting in vibrant colors. I stared at it, again drawn to it. I felt myself yearning for that something which the painting only hinted at, that elusive place of belonging. It made me yearn, made me believe that there was more to life than the yellowed crust I nibbled at.

Naomi's bedroom light was on when I reached her home. Her parents' bedroom was dark; they had already gone to sleep. I laid my bike down at the base of the tree and climbed until I was level with Naomi's room.

Her drapes were drawn, so I couldn't see what she was doing inside. I rapped softly on the window, mindful that her parents were light sleepers. After a half minute, the drapes parted and her face appeared in the window. She was surprised to see me; I signaled her to put a jacket on and pointed upwards toward the apex of the tree.

When we were really young, we used to climb to the very top where the view was incredible. Perched up there, we'd be relatively out of earshot of her parents and could talk freely, taking in the vista of the Ashland night.

She closed the drapes; when they were opened again, she was fully decked out in winter clothing. In her hand was a thermos likely containing some leftover hot-and-sour soup from the Panda House.

We climbed up without saying a word. I let her climb ahead of me, and she moved nimbly, catlike. Even in the dark, I easily followed her, taking hold of grips and convenient footholds I knew were there. The night sky was sprinkled with stars, glittering with abandon. Our breaths coagulated in frosty plumes.

We gazed out at the silver spread of land before us.

"I've never been up here when it's so cold," I said. "Can't even feel my cheeks." I felt less stable up here in the winter; the branches, so warm and coarse in the summertime, were now slicked over with snow and ice. I fastened my right arm hard around a branch.

"There," Naomi said. She was pointing towards a cluster of lights sparkling upon the darkened plains like a tray of diamonds. "The dot of light all by itself over there. That's the school."

"That one?"

"No, that one. Follow my pointed finger."

I angled my head along the trajectory of her arm. "Oh."

We both gazed at the lighted dot for a time. It looked so far away, so impossibly small.

"The police are still there," she said quietly.

"Maybe it's just light from the auditorium. The stage crew's supposed to be working through the night to be ready for tomorrow."

She wiped her nose against the back of her glove, something she did only when she was alone with me. "So, do you think you're ready for it?"

"The performance? I think so. I've done everything I possibly can. Matthewman's been incredible, coaching me. I'm just worried that I haven't even sung with the chorus yet."

"It's so weird to think you have the lead. Still trying to get my mind wrapped around that one."

"You and the rest of the world," I said.

"I didn't mean it that way. It's just that I've never heard you sing before."

"I saved you a ticket," I said, turning to her. "It's third row."

"Xing," she said tentatively, "do you have an extra ticket? I'd like to bring Jason, if I can."

I did not say anything.

Minutes passed. Naomi took out a chocolate bar and offered half to me. I took it. As she chewed, she took out the thermos she'd been keeping under her jacket. "It's Ah-ma and Ah-ba's soup," she told me, and we both drank it eagerly. The heat hummed down into our stomachs. One by one, the lights of the town flickered off until only a few isolated dots of light remained, like the fading embers of a dying campfire.

"I know it bothers you, Xing."

"What does?"

"Don't be like this."

"Like what?"

She patted the branch in front of her. "It just kinda happened so fast, and it was all so...incredible. I would have told you, honestly I would have, but that was around the time when you got really busy with your voice lessons. We didn't see each other a whole lot anymore, we lost touch with each other, and suddenly...I started to spend a lot of time with Jason, and I kind of neglected our friendship." She looked remorseful. "It was my fault. I should have let you know earlier. But I had to deal with my parents, too, who were dead-set against the relationship. There were a lot of disagreements, angry words thrown..." She wiped her eyes. "But I should have told you. I'm sorry, Xing, really I am."

She turned her head away. A sliver of moonlight lined her soft jawbone and full lips.

"Just tell me one thing," I said. "Did you and I...did I ever have a chance of being more to you than just a friend?"

She turned back to me now, and I saw the look of a Naomi she never showed to anyone. It was that of a lost girl, an unsure person, that dependent Naomi who had once clung to my sleeve in school because I was the only person who looked like her, who didn't tease her, who explained things slowly to her. The Naomi to whom I had taught English, those countless hours at the food court. Those innumerable walks to and from school. Rides together on the bus. The letters we wrote to each other, the little comments she'd write on my notebook during class. Movies we had sneaked into, staying there the whole day, jumping from screen to screen. Playing catch on deserted park fields; on the phone till late at night; swimming at deserted ponds in the summer all day; midnight meetings on this very tree, scribbling notes to one another.

When I was young, I had a secret dream. That Naomi would one day live with me permanently in this tree. We would build a huge tree house filled with all the amenities we could possibly want. An entertainment system, game consoles, a pet dog, a food machine capable of generating any dish we commanded it to make. Peking duck. Shark fin soup. Buddha's delight. Congee with a thousand-year-old preserved egg. Our house would be perched so high up, no one would ever dare climb the tree to reach us. And we would never, ever have to leave that tree, not even to go to school. It would be just Naomi and me, just the two of us in the whole world.

"No," she said. "I don't think so."

I wrapped my arms tighter around the branch. I was suddenly certain of one thing. I had to say it or spend my whole life regretting it.

"Naomi." I could hardly hear my own voice. "I love you."

Her eyes teared up, glistening in the moonlight. But even with her tears, I saw that my words were useless, that they were wasted, that I should never have said them. For I almost knew what she was going to say before she said it.

"Xing," she said softly, "you and I have this really special relationship. You are as necessary and as fundamental to my life as anything else I have. I can't imagine living the past eight years without you, how I would have survived. And when I think of the future, I can't picture it without you." She sniffed, swallowed hard. "But if you were to ask me about the possibility of you and me being together in a different way...I'd be lying if I told you I never thought about it. But no. It's not going to happen."

My own eyes welled up; she became a diffused, hazy figure before me. "Nobody will ever love you the way I do," I said. I blinked; tears rolled down my face, and I flicked my head to the side, wiping the tears away. But I had seen it already.

That look on her face. Someone else had already beaten me to it; Jason had already said those words to her. I suddenly knew that over the course of her life, she would have many men express that to her. And I knew, too, that I would now never be remembered as the first to say such words to her. Only the most sincere; and this, my sole, wretched secret.

I stared out into the night.

The air was clear as if every molecule of darkness had been scrubbed clean. I could have thrown a paper plane into the night, and it would have sailed right across the plains to the hills silhouetted against the silvered sky. Naomi's eyes shimmered in the opaque darkness; her cheekbones were luminescent, marred by a faint tiny scar under her left eye. Only a person who knew it was there would notice it.

"Do you remember the first day we met?" I asked.

Her eyes, searching mine, did not comprehend.

"Years ago in elementary school, the day when you were taken to the nurse's room because you were bleeding from a rock thrown at you?" I turned away from her now and spoke in a level tone. "I was asked to come in and translate. That was how we met, Naomi; I don't know if you remember that."

"I remember," she said. Her voice was nothing more than a whisper.

"Some stupid kids had been throwing snowballs at you in the playground, pelting you with them. I remember that," I said, my voice edgier now, louder. "Everyone was laughing at you, mocking you."

"Stop, Xing, please," she pleaded.

"I remember how everyone stopped playing and came to watch. To taunt. The Chinese girl who couldn't speak English. Wearing a Playboy jacket." I breathed in deep.

"Stop."

"But there was also a rock thrown, wasn't there? Did you ever see who threw the rock at you? Did you ever see who reared his arm back and whipped it at you?"

She turned to face me, her eyes widening, disbelieving.

"It was me, Naomi. I was the one who picked up the rock. I was the one who threw it. I threw it as hard as I could at the little Chinese girl who couldn't speak English. I remember how it hit you flush in the face. Right under your left eye. It cut you open. I remember how much I hated you."

Her face contorted in sorrow before me. And just before she turned away, I saw it crumble.

I made my way down the tree, picked up my bike, and rode away. When I reached the bottom of the hill, I turned around and looked for the tree. But it was too dark and there were too many other trees, and after a while I jumped back on the bike and pedaled away.

DECEMBER 23, PERFORMANCE DAY

It was a quarter to eight when I finally woke up. Sunshine poured in through the thin curtains. I'd missed my morning practice—Mr. Matthewman would be gravely worried and was perhaps even now pacing back and forth in the music room, straining to hear my approaching footsteps. I packed my bag quickly, stuffing in the music sheets. Down the stairs. Grabbed my jacket, bolted outside. My legs were stiff as wooden stilts as I ran for the bus. Panting and wheezing from the run, I boarded the bus. Something was different today, though. The bus was packed. Not an open seat in sight. The sky was dark and ominous as the bus chugged its way to school, the radio broadcasting more news about the discovery at the pond. Everyone listened. And eyed me, still standing, trying to find a seat.

Physics, first period. The classroom television turned on. CNN reporting about the bodies. Commercial break. Then short, complimentary life stories of each deceased student.

Naomi sat next to me. Not once did she look my way.

Jan Blair's seat was empty.

About fifteen minutes into class came the sound of approaching footsteps. It was Mr. Marsworth. I gripped the sides of my desk, my knuckles turning white, like snowballs in a ziplock bag. I feared the worst: he was going to cancel the musical. He briefly whispered a few words to the teacher, then addressed the class.

"Good morning, folks." He was all gussied up; his hair was slicked back, shining with gel. "With all that's been going on around town over the last few weeks, and with all that happened last night, I understand that there are a lot of concerns and fears. And there are also some rumors flying around," he continued. "Let me emphasize to you that they are just that—rumors. And I want to put to bed some of these rumors. First, school is not, and will not be, canceled today. And second, the musical will go on." He jutted his chin. "I've spoken to some teachers, some parents. We all agree that the best thing is to go on with it. So please, please bear with us, as we are all doing our very best to stay atop the current situation."

The bell rang.

Just as I was leaving, I saw Mr. Marsworth speaking with the teacher in hushed tones. I made my way quietly towards them.

"...Blair's usually here. Can't remember a time when she wasn't."

"I'll check with Miss Winters," Mr. Marsworth muttered, picking some lint off his new suit. "See if she was in homeroom this morning." His cell phone rang and he walked away, flipping his phone open. His eyes darted back and forth behind his new glasses; he wet his lips, then trotted away, barking into the phone.

If it had been anyone else, I'm sure of it, everything would have come to a stop. Classes would have been cancelled. The evening's performance cancelled, or at least postponed. More police on the scene. But I'm convinced that because it was only Jan Blair —the scraggly castaway—who was unaccounted for, nobody really cared too much. Or enough, which in the end is all that matters.

Mr. Matthewman was in an acrid, bitter mood when I went to see him after first period.

"I know it was under extenuating circumstances. I know it's not every day that dead bodies are pulled out of the pond. I'm trying to be understanding about this! But couldn't she have had you sing earlier in the night?" He slammed his hand down on the piano, and a hum reverberated inside it.

I faltered on my heels, taken aback. "I...it wasn't my place to tell her what to do," I said defensively.

"Kris, do you understand what all this means?" he asked me, clearly exasperated. He ran his hand through his thinning hair. "Do you know what kind of a pickle this puts you in?" he continued, taking me to task.

"Yes. I suppose I do. It just means I'll have to go in cold with the chorus tonight."

"Oh, it most certainly does mean that," he said, barely letting me finish my sentence. "But that's not the problem. You can most certainly adapt to them; you're not the problem. It's them. The chorus. They're the problem. They've never

practiced with you. One little change, and you'll throw them
for a loop. And their amateurish house of cards will coming
tumbling down, just like that. We'll become the laughing-
stock of this pathetic little town!" He banged his hands on
the piano. He finally breathed in deeply and let out a long,
withdrawn sigh. He sat down, defeated. "You have no idea,
Kris. It's become a media circus. Photographers will be there
taking pictures of the 'little children in the little town that
could.' *New York Times, USA Today*, to name a few. America's
youth standing up in the face of evil. The national audience
will eat this up, and the media knows this. They'll be here in
full force."

"You're exaggerating."

He shook his head. "Suddenly all the big shots in town
want to be here, dignitaries. Judges. Businessmen. Even the
mayor, for crying out loud. It's become very political. A mec-
ca for face time." He cleared his voice, his left hand rubbing
his Adam's apple. "Maybe it's my fault. By now I should have
made sure that you've practiced at least three, four times with
the chorus."

"Things happened, though. Things beyond your control.
My mother getting hospitalized."

He nodded, a taut grimace tight-roped across his lips.
"Still. There's more that I could've done." He lifted up the
piano lid and played a few notes. His fingers halted just above
the keys, shaking a little. "Nobody's heard you sing but me.
Nobody knows how good you are. And tonight, it will be
your one and only chance to show the world. That's a lot of
pressure to contend with. I should never have put you into
such a tight corner. Even the worst singing instructor in the
world knows that if you have a real talent, you show him off
before the actual performance, if only to instill confidence

before it really matters. Great word of mouth is a terrific performance enhancer."

"You said I could sing. That's enough for me."

"Me? One person?"

"Yes. Your opinion matters more than this whole town's combined."

He smiled with sadness. "Does it really? Do you know what I am? A burnt-out has-been who threw away a burgeoning career."

"You're a Julliard professor. That's enough for me."

He didn't say anything in response. But tentatively, he turned to the piano, staring down at the keys. He began to play, a yielding piece. Gray hair dappled his uneven sideburns in dotted flecks. He looked older to me than when we'd first started, more strained. The crow's feet at the corners of his eyes looked more canyoned than before.

His fingers, long and bony, took on a life of their own as they stretched across the keyboard and prodded music out of the keys. Calloused skin with bitten fingernails tapped down on the smooth black and white of the keyboard. The back of his hand, a kaleidoscope of jutting bones and green-colored veins intersecting one another. His whole body, moving to the music in muted fashion, radiations of melancholy.

It was a piece I'd never heard before. Not for the first time, I wondered about his past. After so long with him, all I knew of him was his passion for music. There were brief moments—no more than two or three over the many weeks I'd been tutored by him—when I saw his eyes suddenly take on a different quality. But he'd quickly barricade himself behind closed eyelids, and when he opened them, he'd flushed away the strange opacity.

He shrugged. "Well." He looked like he wanted to say more. "Well."

"I'll be ready tonight, Mr. Matthewman. I promise you that."

He nodded slowly at first, then with more energy. "You'll be great, Kris, I know that. If the chorus begins to falter, remember, you'll have to adapt to their fluctuations. They're more of them, and they're all less skilled than you. You'll have to maneuver to match them."

"How do I do that?"

"You'll just know. It's something that can't be taught."

"I need more than that."

"Really, there's nothing more I can say. Just think of it as balance." He gave me an affirming look. "You'll be fine, Kris. I was just overreacting earlier. Just remember everything I've taught you, and you'll be great out there."

I moved over to my bag and took out all my music sheets. "I can't believe it's really happening. In just a few hours. The stage lights coming on. The audience piling in. The cameras snapping. And me, standing in the middle of it all. Not a single dress rehearsal to get me warmed up, used to the idea. And suddenly, right there, in the spotlight. All eyes focused on me. Unbelievable."

He drummed his fingers lightly against the piano stool. "If you get too many butterflies, just close your eyes. Shut out everything else."

"And it's going to happen for sure? The performance?"

"The show will go on."

"How can you be so sure?"

"Mr. Marsworth needs this to happen in the worst way. He's made too many promises, got the media way too involved. Besides," he continued, "I heard something. The police are really close."

"They've been saying that for weeks now."

"Yes, but this time I think it's true. They're close. By tonight, someone was saying. Perhaps even before the performance, they'll nail the perp. If that's the case, the performance can be like a celebration of sorts, the end of this madness."

"But it could be anyone out there! What makes—?"

He cut me off by nodding vigorously. "That's what the police thought. But they're now working under the theory that the abductor is working in-house, so to speak. They ran fingerprint checks against registered parolees, that kind of thing. Zilch. So now they're thinking that it's someone from inside the school. All the circumstantial evidence points that way. A janitor. A teacher. Any one of the administrative staff. It's so obvious when you think about it. An outsider would have been noticed quickly; it has to be someone who can walk around the hallways unnoticed. One of us. Disturbing thought, isn't it? Everyone on payroll at this school— teachers, janitors, secretaries—we all had to go down to the station house yesterday to give our fingerprints. You should have seen us, eyeing each other. Any one of us could be it. Scary thought."

"It could be a student," I told him.

He looked at me with a slanted frown. "You don't really think so, do you?"

I shrugged nonchalantly. "You never know."

We talked for a few minutes more, mostly about the evening's performance. He reminded me to be backstage in the dressing room at five sharp, two hours before the show began.

On my way out, I closed the door of that music room for the very last time, recalling the many lessons, the hours spent in there. They were the happiest of times, the one place where Slackenkill High actually did something good for me. Most of all, I would remember the timbered voice of Mr. Matthewman instructing me, the crisp clarity of the piano notes strident against the wintry gray outside, the lamp atop the piano shining a tent of light, the crackle of music sheets being turned. My voice learning to soar, finding itself, coming back to me off the walls strident and assured: this room, my oasis of possibility. Those last mornings.

For that day alone, I was granted an unprecedented level of freedom at school. Mr. Matthewman had convinced the school that I shouldn't be required to attend the usual classes but should rather be allowed to spend the hours before the show as I saw fit. I was encouraged to spend time in the auditorium, to familiarize myself with the surroundings. Something which, I thought bitterly to myself, should have been done weeks ago.

I made my way to the auditorium. The hallways were scrubbed in anticipation of the media's arrival; in the school foyer, trophies, long atrophying in dust and memory, found new life. Inside the auditorium, there was a hubbub of activity. Mike tests, sound adjustments, last-minute tweaking of the set. I stood unobserved at the back, hidden over in darkness. No one came to speak with me. Even just hours away, it all seemed so unreal, disconnected to me.

For a long time I stared at the stage set, at the very spot where Jan Blair had kissed me. I wanted to get her out of my mind, but her absence at school was bothering me. I found myself becoming preoccupied with her and, like a nagging splinter, suddenly unable to rid myself of her.

Everywhere I looked, her face loomed, ghostly and ephemeral. I saw her on the stage, in the aisle, a few rows down. Her face contorted in pain and tears. Mouth twisted in fear. I shook my head. Yet still her face, twisted and aghast, hovered all around.

Before I knew it, I was opening my locker and removing my jacket. I was going out. I was going to Jan Blair's home.

Perhaps it was the snow, but her home that afternoon looked a lot more welcoming. The dilapidated yard, the shanty roof, the cast-off trash—all of it now lay under a plush blanket of snow that made her place look almost inviting. Not a footprint in the smooth and undisturbed layer of snow outside. Thin trails of smoke strung upwards from a make-shift chimney, the only indication of life inside.

Tucked away in a hidden corner of the woods, the silence here was dense as if all the quiet of the town had slid into this enclave and stratified.

The porch creaked under the weight of my boots. For a moment I paused, considering. And before I had time to reach a decision, the door opened, surprising me. A man— he looked to be in his early thirties—smiled at me. He was pleasant looking, cherubic even, possibly handsome if not for his height. He was shorter than me, reaching no higher than my shoulder. His clothing was the most surprising. Contrary to what Jan Blair wore to school, he was dressed with immaculate cleanliness, in what seemed to be spanking new North Face gear.

"Hello there!" he beamed, taking a quick look behind me. "Here alone?"

I nodded. "I'm sorry to bother you. I was looking for Jan."

"Ah, yes. She just stepped out. For more firewood. Amazing how fast it all burns up."

He gave a winsome smile. "You must be a friend of hers."

"Yes. She wasn't in school today, and since I was just passing by, I thought I'd check in on her."

"Kinda on a spur-of-the-moment type of thing?" he asked.

"Type of thing," I said, nodding.

With surprising quickness, he stuck out a hand. "Jan's father. Jack. It's nice to meet you."

"I'm Kris," I said, shaking his hand. He had a feeble grip, wispy. He let go of my hand with an approving look.

"I know," he said. He must have seen the puzzlement on my face and chuckled pleasantly. "Jan tells me everything."

"Where did she go? Maybe I can go help her," I suggested.

"Don't worry about it. Come in and wait. She'll be back soon enough." He sidestepped to let me through. Then he closed the door behind us.

It had been cleaned up since the last time. The tins and empty cans were gone. The pile of dirty dishes in the sink had been washed, dried, and put away. The furniture now aligned with the contours of the room. Even the cat was gone, from the kitchen, in any case.

"Looks like somebody's been doing a little housecleaning," I said.

"Jan," he responded glumly. "She started cleaning things up this morning. Said it was a pigsty." He shook his head sadly. "She shouldn't have done that."

"Why not?"

"She was a bad, bad, bad girl this morning. I get back after being out all night, I'm tired, tired, tired. Barely recognize this place, it's so clean. She left no stone unturned. Every drawer opened, every nook and cranny dusted and cleaned. Nosing around, snooping all over the place, meddling into my things.

Sometimes I don't know why I bend over backwards so much for her."

"I'm not sure I understand."

"She should have listened. Should have just left things alone. She shouldn't have..." He shook his head swiftly from side to side as if in denial. "It doesn't matter," he said at last.

I looked out the window. "You said she's out there? How long has she been outside?"

Something in him suddenly mellowed. He massaged his neck slowly, his lips upturned at the corners. "What were you thinking, coming out here in the cold? Must be pressing, whatever you came to see Jan about."

"Just...you know. She's never missed a day of school. Just thought to drop by."

"OK," he said cheerfully. He pulled a chair out from the table, its legs squawking against the floor. "Hey, have a seat."

He pulled out another chair across from me and sat down. He was younger than I'd first thought, boyish. But fastidious. The kind of person who would have trimmed his knuckle hairs had he had any. His face, in fact, was completely devoid of any facial hair. A gleaming egg. A shiny, happy, jolly egg.

"Was Jan not feeling well today?"

"Huh?"

"Jan. She wasn't in school today."

"Oh, yes, yes," he said hurriedly, dismissively, "she has a touch of the flu, under the weather, that kind of thing, you know?"

"She's outside, though?"

He smiled, glowing with pride. "She's got spunk, that girl, you know what I mean?"

"Maybe I should go out and help her. If she's got a cold, maybe she shouldn't be out there."

"Don't you want to stay in here?" He looked suddenly hurt. "Are you comfortable?" he asked, concerned. "Are you warm enough? Are you dry? Why don't you take off your jacket? You really should be warm enough in here."

"No, I'm fine. I'm just worried about Jan."

"Don't you worry about her. I'm looking out for her. She and I, we're tight that way," he said. "I look after her. I make sure she's safe. I make sure she has no troubles with nothing and no one."

I studied him a little more closely. "Is it just the two of you out here?"

He flicked his eyes at mine, then just as quickly flicked them away. "There's three of us, actually."

I waited for him to go on. "Who else?" I asked when he didn't elaborate.

"Well, there's me. There's Jan. And now there's you."

I paused, then asked, "Think she'll be back soon?"

A quizzical expression landed on his face. He ignored my question. "You look as if you have a slim build inside all that clothing. Do you?"

I paused. "Excuse me?"

"Don't worry," he said. "There'll be time for that later." He stood up suddenly, showing again the disconcertingly lithe quickness. "Tea?"

"No. No, thank you." I sniffed. Even in the cold air, a muskiness hung, a misplaced stench.

I listened for signs of others in the house. It was quiet.

He came back from the counter, a glass of water in hand. He sat watching it with careful intent, like a hunched cat ready to pounce on an unsuspecting mouse. He faded away; I sensed his mind drifting out the window, floating over the darkening town. His nails were trimmed to nubs; his hands seemed flawless, without a single crease or hair. As if made out of white marble, and as pale. He had Jan's eyes. Other than that, there wasn't much more of a resemblance.

And for the first time, I observed he had a cold. His nose was running, a single streak flowing out of his left nostril down to the tip of his nose where it hung precariously like a teardrop. It dropped, finally, falling into his glass of water. *Blop*. He took a sip.

"Jan's told me all about you." He studied me, then continued when I didn't respond. "Everything. She says you're a good singer, that you like this girl Naomi at school, that you go to church, that you were once chased in the woods. Don't look so shocked; I told you she tells me everything. She even told me that you're a great kisser." He looked at me closely, his eyes traveling down to my lips. "I could have told her that."

I did not say anything.

"She told me you were here a few nights back." He gave a goofy grin. "And you heard me snoring, she said. I get like that when I get tired. And boy, have I been running around all over town. It's fun, get to see all kinds of stuff."

He took a sip of water.

"Do you know what else she told me?" He didn't wait for an answer. "Told me you rejected her, that you called her—" his mouth twisted into a painful grin "—a slut." He shook his head. "You hurt her, you know, when you said that, when you rejected her."

The walls of the room seemed to shift inward. Enclosing me. "I...I..."

"Oh, don't you worry," he said, smiling now. "Jan's a tough girl. She's had it hard so far. She's tough as nails; she'll get through. It's just that..." His smile disappeared. "I don't like it when people hurt her anymore."

"I didn't mean to hurt her."

"Boys hurt her. I tell them to stop. They never do." He looked at me with a whiny expression. "Why won't they stop? Why does it have to come to..." And again his voice trailed off.

Blop. Another drop fell from his nose into the glass of water.

"She's a wonderful person, did you know that? Most people can't see it, can't see how special she is." His tongue snaked out and moistened his lips. "She's done with hurting, I tell you. No more. Crossed the country to give her a new start; no more hurting for her."

Blop.

"Whoever hurts her is dealt with now. I'm not putting up with anything, no more. A mean word, a mean look, a mean anything, doesn't matter, there are consequences now. Daddy is looking out for her now."

"I didn't mean to...maybe she just misunderstood me."

He broke out laughing. "That's what they all say. It's amazing. Each and every one of them. When I have them cornered, when they've lost all hope, they always start to beg and plead and cry and sob. You should hear them. *Oh, I didn't mean to laugh at her. Oh, I didn't mean to tease her about how stupid she is. Oh, I didn't mean to say she sings like a toad. Oh, I didn't mean to punch her.*" His eyes clenched on mine. "*Oh, I didn't mean to call her a slut.*"

For what seemed like an eternity, he held my gaze as if daring me. I pulled my jacket sleeve back and looked at my watch. "Wonder when he'll get here," I mumbled to myself.

"Who?"

"Mr. Matthewman."

"Who's he?"

"Oh, a teacher at school. We were wondering why Jan didn't come to school today. He said he'd drop by to check on her after I told him I was coming here first. Should be here any second, actually. School's so close by."

He looked at me with friendliness twinkling in his eyes; his lips, however, steely and knotted, sneered. "I thought you said you came here on the spur of the moment," he said, "just as you were passing by."

"Oh, you know. In a manner of speaking."

"'In a manner of speaking,'" he mimicked back at me, his voice high-pitched and affable. "Kids these days. Think they're all so high and mighty." He stared at me, his cheeks, now rosy, pliable as margarine. "'In a manner of speaking.' Why can't you just speak plain English? 'In a manner of speaking.' What the hell kind of English is that?"

He glared at me, disgust raging in his eyes now. He shook his head, suddenly slapping himself with a vicious slap. Again, with that disconcerting speed. The sound resonated around the room. When he looked back at me, his eyes were moist, his face soft, friendliness emanating from him once again. "Would you like some tea?"

"No."

"Are you warm enough?"

I nodded.

"Do you want to take off your jacket? Make yourself comfortable?"

"I'm OK."

"I bet you're very skinny," he continued, barely waiting for an answer, "like all Orientals are." He cast a careful look at me. "You know, you speak really good English for an Oriental."

The chair under me creaked.

"I'm very good at differentiating between Orientals, as a matter of fact," he continued. "Many people have difficulty distinguishing between Koreans, Japanese, and Chinese;

but for me it's never been a problem." He leaned back, concentrating. "Koreans have rounder faces with big, protruding cheekbones. Japanese have narrow eyes, pointed noses. Chinese have stubbier noses, wider faces." He looked at me. "Don't you find that to be true?"

"I don't—"

"'In a manner of speaking.'" He giggled. "Say, 'In a manner of speaking.'"

Then I heard it. The smallest of sounds coming from down the short hallway. A minuscule scratching sound. Then it ceased.

The room fell into a silence. Outside, snow began to fall in thick columns, darkening the interior of the house even more.

"Well, I best be going now," I said, trying to keep my voice steady.

"Whatever do you mean by that?" he asked leaning forward. The smell of toothpaste floated over to me. "You just got here."

"Jan's not here. I should go."

"Don't be silly. Relax." He smiled.

I looked down. Pools of melted snow had gathered around my boots, darkening the wood floor.

He looked at me studiously. "You're Chinese, aren't you?"

I didn't answer.

He smiled at me. "I've never had a Chinese before."

I leapt up and bolted for the door.

He responded with cheetah-like quickness.

Even before my chair—sent flying as I jerked upwards—smacked against the wall, he was lunging across the table at me. His fingers grazed against the front of my jacket, but that was all he got.

I pushed off and moved towards the door, each step a maddeningly slow plod.

His failed lunge stalled him. But not for long. I felt him gathering himself, leaping towards me even as I reached for the door.

I got maybe seven or eight strides outside, felt my speed gathering under me, my boots kicking out well against the snow, feeling a sudden surge of power and belief—

When I felt his fingers grip around my neck.

I screamed as he pushed me facedown into the snow.

The air was knocked out of me. I tried to curl, but his body fell atop mine. He grabbed my hair and sledgehammered my head into the ice-hard ground. My vision went red. He slammed my head down again; my vision blurred. I cried out. His hands gripped my hair anew; then I heard the sound of hair being ripped out by its roots. My head was shoved down again, skull slammed; I almost blacked out. My body collapsed on the ground, sagged heavy about me.

He picked me up like a rag doll and slung me over his shoulder. He made little fuss. He walked back into the house; his boot prints in the snow were small, that of a little boy playing with glee and abandon in the winter's first snow. Delicate, prissy prints. A slight hum escaped his lips.

He believed me to be unconscious.

He dumped me like a sack of potatoes on the kitchen floor. It took everything I had to stifle a yelp of pain. I felt him staring down at me, observing. I hid behind my mask of unconsciousness, evened my breathing. A cold draft scrabbled along the floorboards with the smell of wet cat hair. He stood over me as if claiming me, then he walked away, his small, limber feet swishing like a geisha's, barely audible even on the aged, creaky floorboards. I heard him opening drawers in the room down the hallway, the clink of metal clipping through the stillness. Cold, grating, precise sounds, that of a surgeon lining up his tools on a metal tray. The sound terrified me.

I lay for a long time. I could have made a break for it then, I suppose. But my head was swimming and pounding, I barely felt my legs under me, and I knew, with his scissor-snip quickness, any attempt to escape was futile.

Finally I collected my feet under me and stood up, praying that none of the boards would creak. He believed me to be out cold. The element of surprise was on my side now, and I would take him out with a swift stab of a knife.

If only a knife were to be found. The counters and tabletop were completely bare; all the knives must have been moved to the back room. I could hear him sorting through them at a leisurely, meditative pace.

I stared out the window. Through the descending drifts of gray snow, I could just barely make out the surrounding woods. It looked a million miles away in the darkening dusk. Before I could give it another thought, I edged my way down the hallway.

Ten more steps.

The snow suddenly intensified, plummeting down now in fierce droves outside.

Five more steps.

It was darker along the hallway; I splayed my hands out in front of me.

Two more steps.

And then I was in the back room.

His back was to me, broad and hefty, stooped over a table. He was humming softly, which was why he didn't hear me approach. I stepped right up behind him—if he took a step back he would have stumbled into me—and slowly reached forward for a hunting knife just to the right of him. He was so short; bent over, his head came up no higher than my stomach. My fingertips landed on the cold sting of the blade.

In biology class, I had once vomited when I made the first incision into a swollen, formaldehyde-drenched rat. It had taken me five minutes to scrounge up the courage before I took the first flimsy snip. Seconds later, I threw up in the lab sink. Naomi had to complete the whole dissection alone while I watched from a few feet away.

In my mind's eye, I saw my hand moving with one swift movement up towards his soft neck. I saw the blade slicing true and deep.

"Up already?" he asked cheerfully.

I blinked. Swiped for the knife. But too late. It was already in his hand.

He turned around almost casually with a pearlescent smile on his face as if to tell me that everything was all right. "I thought I'd knocked you out cold."

I stepped back, my legs wobbling under me.

"You're more resilient than the other ones," he said matter-of-factly. He looked up and down the length of the blade. "Why did you want this knife?" He frowned, looking at me. "Did you want me to do it *now*?" His face scrunched up even more, a whiny, pinched expression. "But it's way too early for that."

He took a step towards me. I retreated one stride, then two, was about to spin and book when I noticed the pile of blankets cast off to the side. It was wrapped around a little girl, pasty skinned and with closed eyes. Jan. There was a large welt on her cheekbone, a prune-sized shiner encircling her left eye.

"She's been a bad girl," he said, observing that I'd noticed her. "Suddenly starts cleaning the house. It's been just fine all this time, then suddenly she's too good for this place. Starts cleaning up. Starts asking me pesky questions when I get back this morning. 'What are these knives for, Daddy? Where did you get this red jacket from, Daddy? Where do you go at night, Daddy?'"

Jan's eyes suddenly fluttered, trying to open. He didn't notice but ranted on. "'Do you have something to do with the disappearances, Daddy?' she asks. 'Do you this, do you that, do you this, do you that...'" Then, suddenly looming, he shouted, "Doesn't she know I'm looking out for her? Doesn't she know that I'm trying to protect her, trying to give her a new start? Why does she have to make me hit her? Didn't she get hit enough by other boys? Didn't she get hurt bad enough by them?" He gestured wildly with the knife in his hand. "Doesn't she know how much I'm protecting her?"

His eyes fastened on me.

"Protecting her from people who think they're smarter than her."

He took a step towards me.

"From people who think they sing better than her."

He was clutching the knife in his left hand.

"From people who paw her, grope her, touch her."

His nostrils were flaring now, his face flushed with red heat.

"From people who kiss her."

He took another step towards me, spittle flecked on his chin.

"From people who think they're too good for her."

He reared his arm back.

I turned to run.

He was after me already.

I made it to the hallway, the longest hallway in the world, and my boots—clamoring for grip, for distance—thudded halfway down its endless length when—

Only one person in the world knows what happened next, and even then, I'm not entirely sure.

What I do remember is tripping over my own boots. My fleeing body was already at the door twenty feet away, my whitened hands already reaching for the doorknob, my terrified mind already outside, already running into the sanctuary of the town police station, but my boots...

...were still anchored in a terrible slowness, still plodding along the planks of the hallway. Then...they banged into each other, the heel of one boot clipping the tip of the other. And then I was falling. And then I was on the floor.

My fall, so sudden and unexpected, surprised him.

He tripped over me, his nimble feet catching on the back of my thigh.

I remember glancing upwards, seeing a dark form sail over me like a rain cloud. It crashed with a thud a few feet away, shaking the boards. I thought I heard a wheezing sound, then the release of air like a balloon let go. He had impaled himself on the knife he was holding, right through the Adam's apple.

His arms and legs flopped as if trying to swim through the floor.

Then he stopped moving altogether.

★

I crouched down beside Jan, my fingers shaking. Her breathing was rapid and shallow. I reached for her hand.

Freezing. There were bruises around her neck; pockmarks of purple and reddish lacerations marred her skin.

I picked up a blanket from the floor and placed it over her shoulders. Her bangs lay plastered against her cheekbone from dried tears and blood. Gently, I brushed them back and tucked them behind her ear. For a second, her eyes opened partway at me through the stipple of bruises and welts. She had arresting green eyes, depth and soul. I'd known this since the very first time our eyes had met in the classroom so many weeks before.

Then her eyes closed again.

I carried her. I could not leave her there alone. So I took my jacket off, wrapped her in it, and somehow found the strength to lift her. Outside the snowfall had halted, and in that momentary reprieve, I trudged through the snow, through the woods, onto Route 19. I was tired and spent but never stopped. I carried Jan through the dark side of the Ashland dusk along empty roads and quiet streets:

—over the bridge where by tradition high school graduates jumped off in their black gowns into the sun-dappled water sparkling below, yelling with all the delirium of sheer zest and exuberance, their whole lives spread before them with endless possibilities;

—past the local park where Little League games were played in the summer, sunshine pouring down on uniforms bleached impossibly white, picnic mats laid out, beer cans guzzled, oversized women splayed on pool chairs like beached whales, *Good eye, Billy,* and *Atta boy!* being hooted;

—by the corner where a convertible full of tank tops and bikinis and burnt red skin roared past a Chinese boy standing just feet away, making him gasp with wet shock as the car splashed water from the corner puddle onto him, high-fives and derisive giggles trailing along;

—past the corner on that isolated road where a little Chinese boy had once stood dumbfounded, trying to find his daddy, as a dented car made its quick getaway;

—down Main Street now, where in the summer young packs of teenage boys milled around groups of teenage girls, making fun of the little Chinese boy who walked past them, kicking him in the rump, laughing like hyenas;

—and all the way to Fexter Street, where I turned left and walked into the fifth precinct.

For a few seconds I went unnoticed. A uniformed officer at the front desk was busy chatting to what looked like a reporter. On my left, sleeping on the bench was a cameraman, his camera embraced in his arms like a teddy bear. I walked past the front desk, past the elevators on the left, past a *Missing* poster where the faces of Anthony Hasbourd, Winston Barnes, and Trey Logan stared out at me.

I pushed through a set of doors marked *Authorized Personnel Only* and into a room filled with police officers. It didn't take long after that. I heard the scraping of chairs, saw shock-faced officers standing up, wariness and caution all at once. I stood perfectly still, my arms heavy from carrying Jan.

Snow on my clothes and boots flowed down in melted rivulets. I saw my reflection in the mirrored window behind the officers. I was wispy, ethereal, shivering in my sweatshirt, barely holding on to Jan, her arms dangling limp like willows.

"What the hell is this?" an officer asked, his voice gruff with uncertainty and fear.

I wavered a little on my feet. "We've been hurt," I answered.

PERFORMANCE

hat I remember most about that night are the
headlights. I do not remember so well the frenzy
that ensued at the police precinct, nor the statement I later made in a room full of detectives and sergeants.
Only vaguely do I remember Jan being taken from my arms,
carted away into an ambulance. There are hurried snippets of
images that come to mind: the spill of reporters into the press
room, the flashing of light bulbs, being taken away to another
room, the mayor, who personally came down to congratulate
me on finding the killer. The smell of garlic and wine on his
breath as he spoke, his doting hand on my shoulder, pressing,
asking if I was well enough to still perform at school: *Think
about the community, what's best for the community. It would be best
for the community for the show to go on.* The mayor's heated argument with a police sergeant. Cups of hot soup. Coffee. More
questions about what happened. Then being driven to school.

The headlights. Still so ripe in my memory. Sitting in
the dressing room at school, alone at last, staring quietly
out the window, at the approaching headlights. A stream
of luminescent beads bobbling, like phosphorescent paper
boats floating down a brook, journeying towards school.
They were all coming to see me. Perhaps, I imagined,

even Mr. Dan Foss, the owner of a deli downtown who had known me for years yet never addressed me by name like he did the other teens; or Mrs. Tina Shiva, my elementary school teacher who never once called on me to read aloud during the class read-a-thon; Mrs. Patrice Hudson, the town librarian who always eyed me with suspicion; Mr. Thomas Dooling, the owner of a small donut store who once tried speaking to me in a mimicry of Chinese, slapping his buddies when my face went blank and dumb. And many more, all of them now coming to see me. The auditorium lights would dim down, silencing the din of the audience, exposing a single, solitary spotlight pinpointed onto the stage. And then I would step into that beam, and they would be forced to watch me, for there would be nothing else to see; and they would be forced to listen to me, for there would be nothing else to hear; and they would be amazed, astounded, for there would be no other way to respond to my singing.

When I was informed there were only five minutes to go, I exited the changing room. Just outside my room were all the extras and chorus members lined up against the corridor walls decked out in their costumes: prostitutes, tax collectors, shepherds, angels, kings, sheep. They'd been talking in hushed tones, but when I came out they stopped and stared. Word had already gotten around. The serial murderer had been found and killed; I had something to do with it. From behind their masks and dark hoods, they stared out at me. Then a hand stuck out towards me.

"Hey, Kris, go get 'em," said one of the three kings, whom I recognized as Dave Brady, captain of the lacrosse team, who'd never said a word to me before. It was a wonder he even knew my name.

"Yeah, knock 'em dead, Kris," said another voice, and another hand shot toward me. And with that, a chorus of voices spoke, encouraging me. More hands extended toward me to shake my hand or to slap me on the back or shoulder in support. It was all new to me. For the next ten seconds, I walked down the length of the hallway, shaking hands, nodding my head, grinning from ear to ear. I suddenly felt more alive than I ever had, as if my life were only now truly beginning. My skin, slightly clammy, prickled in the cool backstage air; my heart kicked with the prospect of new birth.

I heard the audience begin to clap and, soon after, Mr. Marsworth start speaking. He spoke ingratiatingly, welcoming the dignitaries in the audience. The chorus, stagehands, and musicians moved as one, as quietly as possible, taking position backstage behind the thick velvet curtains. Marsworth droned on, speaking of the fire of suffering which helped to meld the town into a more united one. There was thunderous applause at that. Dripping with smarminess, he spoke of the teachers at the school, of their efforts at making this evening's performance the pinnacle of what the town of Ashland was all about, namely excellence and perseverance in the face of adversity and evil. He punctuated his speech with exclamations that jangled the mike into shrieks of feedback, but he seemed oblivious. The audience was rapturous to give praise that night and responded heartily as he waxed eloquent. At long last, he ended his speech to deafening applause and stepped off the stage. The lights began to dim, submerging all of us backstage into darkness.

I was suddenly terrified, realizing I'd made a gargantuan mistake. The audience out there was ravenous, an untamed beast, hungry to tear to shreds its prey. I never imagined that it could be so loud, so alive, squirming and writhing before me in the throes of its own heated passion. Singing to

Mr. Matthewman in the safe confines of the music room was wholly different from what was before me here.

The music began. I ducked back further backstage, behind some of the sheep. The curtains opened, and light poured onto the stage like water bursting from a dam. This was it then. The moment had arrived. And I was not ready; I was not prepared for this. The applause was rawer and more visceral than ever.

The sheep in front of me bobbed up and down in eager excitement. I saw one of them lean over and whisper, "This is freaking awesome!" All the sheep nodded their heads in agreement. The shepherds walked onstage, taking their positions. There was a brief pause in the music; then the baton came down, the orchestra played, and the chorus of shepherds began to sing. The musical had, for better or for worse, begun. Not in a million years would I ever be ready for this. I was insane to think that I could ever pull it off. My frayed nerves turned my head into a frightened, swimming mush; my voice was stuck in quicksand a thousand miles away. I wanted to curl up and disappear.

The first number ended. The audience clapped long and hard. The stagehands flew onto the stage, carrying off the well, moving in some trees and a placard board horse. The lights came on, and the sheep came waddling on, much to the cheers and amusement of the audience. It was an audience-friendly song, this one, and they ate up the easy rhythm and occasional bleating sounds coming from the sheep. Even in my frenzied state of mind, I knew that the show was going well—every number had been performed to perfection. Even Miss Jenkins was smiling approvingly backstage, her arms clasped around a clipboard in an amorous embrace.

I watched as the sheep came offstage, high-fiving one another, smiling in a celebratory mood, the stagehands once again rushing out. My moment had arrived.

The lights became muted, and I took my place at the side of the stage, refusing to look out at the audience. It had gone quiet; it had not been this silent the whole night. I saw the last stagehand put a large potted plant in the back and scamper off, head tucked down. Then I felt a slight nudge on my back, and Miss Jenkins's voice whispered, "Now."

And so, at long last, the moment arrived. I walked out to center stage, hearing Miss Jenkins hissing out last orders. Then even her voice faded. Then it was just me standing in the middle of the stage, alone.

Mr. Matthewman, conducting at the top of the orchestral pit, made eye contact with me; I closed my eyes. I wasn't ready. *For a few more seconds*, I thought to myself, *just a few more seconds, I can keep my eyes closed.* I stood very still. Slowly I cracked open my eyes to the auditorium before me. All the world spilled towards me in a hazy gray. Their faces, indifferent and aloof all these years, now were ready to exult me, raise me up, paint me in colors of gallantry, a hero. But on their terms, always on their terms. I'd lived as nothing more than a canvas before them; upon me they would paint whatever they wanted to, whatever colors they chose, whatever imagery they imposed. They would see only the painting they brushed on this compliant, subservient canvas; their eyes would never delve past that thin veneer. But there was more to me than just a canvas. There were secret layers.

I wanted to cry out to the world, "Stop!" For everything to rewind, to somehow be given a chance to go back. And what I would do is go back a week and practice singing on this stage every day. And what I would do is study more, at-

tend church more, become a Christian, become even better
at being a white Christian than Jason ever could. To never
have kissed Jan Blair. And what I would do is journey back
to the time I went to Chinatown with my father, and I would
stay with him the whole time, never have deserted him, and
we would have caught an earlier train home and completely
avoided that skidding car. What I would do. What I would
change. So many things.

I opened my eyes to an unraveled world before me.

Mr. Matthewman was looking at me with steady eyes. He
raised his baton, paused, then let it fall. The music began.
The spotlight splashed all over me. I never blinked.

Alone onstage, I lifted my head up to the light and released my voice, not knowing what would come out. And
what flowed out was a voice I'd never heard before: not the
tilted croak of nervousness, nor the menagerie of beauty
formed in Mr. Matthewman's music room. This was something altogether different: passionately raw, wrenchingly incandescent. As I sang, I traveled to places I never wanted to
go. Where a heart broke with the grief of unrequited love.
Where hollowed-out eyes turned upwards to empty skies
above. To the widest, most open expanse of a land of utter
emptiness and loneliness. My voice rose up to the upper ban-
ners and spread from row to row, passing from person to person like a pale chiffon ribbon billowing across every cheek. A
subtle caress.

A baby who had been fussing in the back row stilled; Mr.
Marsworth stopped chewing gum. I felt every eye fixated on
me, including my mother's, just a few rows from me, wet
with the thought of possibilities lost, never to be retrieved.
And I heard all of them, too, even as I sang. I heard them.
Like so many years ago in that blackened ship, I heard their
whispery voices, pleading in the darkness: "Autumn Moon

on the Calm Lake." "The Glow of the Setting Sun on the Lei Fong Pagoda." "Orioles Singing in the Willows." "Snow on the Broken Bridge." "Evening Knell on the Nan Ping." "Viewing Fish in Huagang."

Limber and supple, my voice swirled around the auditorium.

> O holy night, the stars are brightly shining;
> It is the night of the dear Savior's birth!
> Long lay the world in sin and error pining,
> Till He appeared and the soul felt its worth.

At the song's close, my voice lilted past the fading echo of the stringed instruments. Then the auditorium was hushed over in pure silence.

Then the sound of one person clapping. Then another, and another, until I could no longer distinguish between them. It was the roar of a waterfall. And I saw the audience rise as one, clapping louder than I'd thought possible in this auditorium, vociferous and manic. Cameras reawakened now, clicking madly, their flashbulbs blinding me. Mr. Matthewman, his face percolating with redemption, with release, nodded at me, his hand closed in a triumphant fist.

And my mother. Almost lost in the audience, her face hovered like a surreal mirage, hands clasped together at her chin. Glowing with something like pride, feeling something like hope. For a brief moment, before she was swallowed up by the crowd, our eyes met. It seemed like the first time in years that we'd looked at each other. Really saw each other. There was tenderness, there was regret in her eyes.

And that's where I'll stop. Whenever I remember this night, I always stop here. Standing on stage, my eyes filled to the brim, flashbulbs popping around me like strobe lights, the clatter of incessant clapping ringing in my ears, and the feeling deep inside me that this was the zenith of my life, that nothing could ever, ever top this transcendent moment.

MASK

Years ago, when I was nine, my parents permitted me to go trick-or-treating without supervision. Certain prohibitions were placed on me, of course. Never was I to go into anyone's home; never was I to sample any of the food or candy given to me, especially not apples; never was I to leave the immediate neighborhood; and never was I to separate from Naomi.

It was all very technical, and soon forgotten. Naomi and I—both costumed in Casper the Friendly Ghost outfits (bought at Wal-Mart, two for the price of one)—ranged the streets, sucked on candy, ripped open chewing gum packs, stepped into strangers' homes. It was never our conscious intent to break the rules, but once out in the streets, the parade of costumes, the beckoning lights, and the giggling masses of children swept us away as in a stream. Only the last instruction was never broken. We never strayed more than an arm's length from each other the whole night.

At some point we joined a group of other children. We didn't know who they were; we all wore masks, spoke in the feigned, caricatured voices of our costumes. Nor did it seem important for us to know. We moved as one from house to house. Even at my young age, I sensed a rhythm, a cadence to all we did. Walk up to the door. Ring the doorbell. The door opens: a blustery woman, all made up with bright mascara and moussed hair, feigns surprise and glee at the sight of us. "Trick or Treat!" we shout in unison. The hands dipping into the bag, friendly admonishments to be careful, closing of the door, then moving on to the next house, to be repeated all over again, house after house.

I remember it so clearly. The hollow, bellowing sound of my voice from behind the mask, the warm condensation collecting there. The two pinpricks on the mask through which I viewed the world, so blessedly small and obscuring. I remember the way they all looked at me as they asked who I was. Every time they asked, I'd intone the voice of Casper the Friendly Ghost, revealing nothing more. *I'm Casper the Friendly Ghost!* I'd see the response in their laughter, so free and unabashed. They never guessed it was a Chinese boy in a white costume.

As I moved about the neighborhood that night, I suddenly knew what it was to be white. I saw smiles and looks never before directed at me. Oh, there had been smiles and there had been friendly looks before, but never so unforced or natural. I understood then what it meant to be of likeness in America, of sameness, to be free from stilted inflections, pondering stares, strained openness. It was the unabashed simplicity of it all, the unbridled acceptance in their blue and green eyes, in their words, which struck me most.

That night, exhausted but exhilarated in my own bed, I hid Casper's mask. After my parents tucked me in and closed the door, I took out the mask from beneath the blankets. It was crumpled by then, but no matter. Even in the dark, its whiteness glowed, its smile shone. I put it on, relishing the splendid anonymity it gave me. And like that, I fell asleep. I dreamed that the mask melded into my face, became immovable, became my face. It was a wonderful dream. To live behind a white mask.

A REVELATION

Backstage, I retreated to my changing room. Miss Jenkins, after hugging me, told me I had about ten minutes before my next number. "You're a revelation," she gushed before closing the door. I turned off the light, needing to gather myself. Even from behind the closed door, I could hear the applause, still thunderous. Sitting down, I rubbed my temples with my thumbs. My heart was thumping, pounding.

And that's when I noticed something peculiar far off: the blinking red and blue dots. From outside the window. Heading towards school, a line of police cars, urgency pulsating in each swivel of red-blue-red-blue lights.

For a minute I stared at them, my curiosity piqued.

There was a loud knock on my door, startling me.

"Yes?" I asked.

"You OK in there?"

"Fine."

"You've got about five more minutes."

"OK." Footsteps receded; I turned back to the window. The distant swirl of red and blue lights, gathering speed, spiraling towards school. And then I heard it. From just outside my door, in the hallway where jackets and backpacks were lined up against the walls. A cell phone started to ring, a muffled melody. Then another. And another. Within a minute, at least a dozen cell phones must have gone off. Something was happening. My fingernails dug deep crescent indentations into my palms.

I opened the door cautiously. No one out there. But cell phones were ringing off the hook with an overlapping frenzy. They cast glowing blurs where they shone through the pockets of bags and coats. I walked over to a bag and took a phone out of the side pocket. It vibrated in my hand like a shivering rat. I waited for it to stop moving. Then I flipped it open and pushed the button for voice mail.

"Listen, Susan, it's Dad. Call me as soon as you get this. It's important. Don't go anywhere, just call me right back."

I put the phone back and fished out another one.

"Harry, word just broke out, you need to call me immediately. Stay with Dad at school, don't stray off alone. They think they know who did it, some kid at school. I don't have—nobody knows for sure, details just came out and are fuzzy. Just find Dad, OK, and stay with him. I'm calling your school now…"

The next phone didn't have a voice message. But the text message screamed at me:

OMG ITS THE CHINESE KID! STAY AWAY FROM HIM…THE GIRL TOLD THE COPS HE DID IT!

I flipped closed the cell phone. It snapped shut like a steel-jaw trap and clattered to the floor.

Time slowed. Then sped forward, then spun around. I started to sway, and I grabbed the wall for balance. The cell phones: they rang with increasing urgency, their lights flashing brighter, electronic beeps now entering the cacophony. And the hallway was suddenly claustrophobic and condemning, as if its thousand million atoms became eyeballs that stared at me with wide-eyed accusation. Then I heard the sound of the audience's laughter from the auditorium gushing down the hallway, shrill and unnerving. As if the walls had become see-through and they were all observing me from their seats, giddy with laughter. At my fear, at my panic.

I walked back into my changing room. I closed the door and sat down. Better in here, away from the phones.

I had nothing to fear. This is what I told myself. Nothing whatsoever. Even if Jan had come to and told the police some lie. A false accusation. That I had attacked her, that I had killed her father. All I had to do was tell the truth. Surely the police would see through her lies.

I stared out at the approaching police cars. The cops had to be coming here only out of mere formality. Not because they believed her. But just for show. To look competent and meticulous in front of all the media. That had to be it. They'd talk to me after the show ended, then shake my hand, tell me, "Great job, Kris, you brought the house down; you're a real hero," and leave. Just a formality. I closed my eyes and forced myself to breathe. Glanced out the window again.

More police cars suddenly, pouring down the road. With alarming speed. And then, even through the closed window, I began to hear the faint blare of sirens.

This was not a formality.

This was an arrest.

I picked up my music sheets and forced my eyes to look at them. *Just concentrate on the next song,* I told myself. *In a few minutes I'll be on stage, and all this will be a silly memory.* But when I looked down, instead of seeing musical notes, I saw, floating between the notes and bars, the image of a gravity knife. *The* gravity knife. The knife Jan had secretly put in my bag as a gift, the one later seized from me and sealed in an evidence bag. The knife that was likely stained with Dorsey's and Hasbourd's and Logan's blood.

And I saw an image of Jan as well, propped up on a hospital bed, spewing lies about me to a receptive audience of detectives and reporters and doctors and nurses. All of them, their heads bobbing up and down, scribbling notes, running out with their cell phones flipped open, fingers punching out text messages.

The crunching sound of tires on gravel outside. My eyes snapped away from the music sheets. The police cars had arrived. So fast. They were chomping at the bit to arrest me. To be able to lead me out, the sicko China boy, on national TV. It was going to be a media Cirque du Soleil with the networks already here filming the show. And the police wouldn't wait for the show to be over. They were coming for me now.

I shook my head fiercely at this. Determined, I stood up, my hand reaching for the hat I would wear for the next number. I rammed it onto my head. Then, after a moment, I righted it. Breathed in, slowly, deeply. I stared at myself in the mirror. *It's OK*, I told myself, *everything is OK*. I went through the first two lines of the next song in my head. For a moment, it seemed possible. To collect myself, to walk out onto the stage, to go on with the performance.

But then I opened the door and fled.

Through the backstage, left towards the janitor's room, then through the back door into the rear parking lot. Not a soul out there, just the cold night and a parking lot full of cars gleaming like the onyx surface of a pond.

I bent down beside a bike rack and found an unlocked bike. Muffled orchestra music seeped out of the auditorium. I stared back at the door. Any moment now. It would bang open. Blue uniforms would push me down into the icy ground, pin my arms painfully behind me.

I cut across the soccer fields to avoid the main roads, my feet piston-like on the pedals. My arms bounced on the handlebars, the uneven field jostling me. The wind sliced through me, tearing my chest into ribbons, filing away at my exposed knuckles. When I reached the woods, I looked back. The auditorium, with light spilling out onto the dark fields, sat like a dropped Chinese lantern.

Ten minutes later, my breath pluming out in front of me in ragged clouds, I broke into a clearing. The road before me was empty. Route 19. Ghosts of snow blew across its length. I pushed on, ignoring the tears that froze in diagonal lines across my cheekbones. Wind slashed through my skin pores, scraping me.

"Please be home, Naomi," I whispered to myself. "Please be home."

She was in the living room, on the phone, her back to me. I watched from outside the window, making sure her boyfriend wasn't with her. She was tense, the earpiece jammed flush against her ear. I watched as she hung up the phone and turned around. Her face was ashen with shock and disbelief.

I walked up the empty driveway—her parents were still working at the mall—and rang the front doorbell. She opened it quickly and let me in without hesitation.

"Oh, my God, Xing, what's going on?" she stammered.

I closed the door behind me. "Listen—"

"I've been hearing crazy stuff."

"Please, Naomi, please you have to—"

"I was just on the phone with Jason. He told me not to let you in if you came—"

"—just listen to me—"

"—he said everyone's calling everyone about it. That you just took off in the middle of the show—"

"—I need you to hear me out. Naomi! *Naomi!*"

That last word came out almost as a scream. It stunned both of us into silence.

"Listen, Naomi," I said, "that's why I rushed over here. I wanted you to hear from me first. Before it all broke out."

Quieter now, but her voice still edged with fright, she said, "Jason told me Jan Blair came to at the hospital. And that she claims you tried to kill her after you killed her father. All sorts of crazy nonsense out there." She started to pace, her hands cupping her temples. "I can't process all this. You're supposed to be performing at school right now. What are you doing *here?*"

I stared blankly at her, trying to find words, some kind of explanation. My chest was rising and falling, still trying to catch my breath.

"It's a mistake, Naomi. It's all just a misunderstanding!"

"I know that! Of course it's a misunderstanding."

"There's an explanation for all of this."

"Of course there is. And you *should* be explaining it. But to the police. Not here, not to me. Now you have the whole world thinking you're guilty. Don't you get it? By running away, you just come off as guilty. Why did you run?"

"Like I've been trying to tell you, I needed you to hear it from me." I ran my hand through my hair in frustration. "They were bearing down on me at school. They were go-ing to put cuffs on me, whisk me away, who knows what after that. I'd never have this moment, just you and me, to explain—"

"You're an idiot, Xing, for coming here. The police were probably going to school to protect you. They knew that false rumors were coming out, and they were just there to ensure your safety." She threw her arms in the air. "How stupid could you be? What possessed you to leave and come here?"

"I needed to tell you I have nothing to do with the killings."

She slapped her thigh in exasperation. "Are you out of your mind?" Frowns of frustration creased her forehead. "Did you really believe I'd think *you* were responsible? Like I would think *you* killed those boys? I'm the last person in the world who needs to be convinced."

We faced each other, confusion-anger-panic churning in the air.

I walked to the window and took a quick glance outside. No one. Yet. "Do you remember that time when we were walking back from school? You were joking about how I was your number one suspect?"

"I was *kidding*, Xing. You can't be serious—"

"I know you were. But it still shows you how easily I fit the profile. I slip into it so perfectly, if you want me to." I sighed angrily. "And they do want me to."

"Look, I'll go down to the precinct with you. I'll do the talking if you want. That this is all just one huge misunderstanding."

"You still don't get it, do you? I'm everything the police could possibly want in a suspect: mysterious, strange, a loner. Discovered only after diligent police work dug up hard-to-find evidence."

"Evidence? What evidence?"

"All circumstantial. Just the worst luck in the world," I said. "Really bad timing, wrong-place-at-the-wrong-time kind of thing. But the evidence is beginning to stack up against me by the minute. Stuff you don't even know about yet."

"What are you talking about? Look, you were almost a victim, for crying out loud." Her eyes pleaded with mine as she spoke. "You can just stop all this paranoid talk. They have the killer. He's dead. He's a cold corpse on the floor with a knife in his neck. You caught him. You put him away. You're a hero, Xing, a—"

"What they have," I interrupted, shaking my head, "is the dead body of a frail munchkin, the kind of person who'd bruise after a mosquito bite. A shrinking violet who looks like the furthest thing from *serial killer*. And then they have me," I said, jabbing a finger at my chest. "Look at me. *Look at me!*" I shouted, jolting her. "Don't I just look the part? Inscrutable, an outcast, foreign, the closest thing to *serial killer*. Because they *will* take the word of even a Jan Blair over mine."

"No, they won't—"

"They have my boot prints!" I shouted. "All over Jan Blair's home, her yard—"

"That's because you were there today! The police know that already—"

"No, just listen to me. I was also there a few days ago."

"What?" She suddenly paused, as if remembering something. "What were you doing there?"

I shook my head, ignoring her. "And motive, too. Perfect motives for at least two of the victims…"

"You're rambling now. Just calm down. Stop thinking the whole world's out to get you."

"You see, Anthony was the one person between me and the lead role. And the Logan kid? Everyone knows we got into a fight. And Winston Barnes? Got me there! But the police are persistent. They'll come up with a motive. Let me try to guess. Maybe it was jealousy. Over how you and Winston were getting along, how he might have replaced me as your study partner." I gritted my teeth. "And then there's the knife—"

Naomi stepped closer to me and placed her hand on my arm. "Xing, stop it!" she said urgently. "You're paranoid; it's not the way you think it is. Nobody hates you the way you think they do. They'll believe you—"

"No, they won't!" I barked at her, and the force of my voice whipped her hand away. "You don't live in my world. You don't know what it's like to walk in my skin, do you?" I was seething now. "They *will* make me into a killer if they want to! Because they've always made me into whatever they want me to be. That's the way it's always been, this school to me, this town to me!"

She took a step back from me, her eyes widening. "How did you get to be like this, Xing? That you see an enemy in every shadow? That you distrust everyone, that you think the worst of them all?"

My face twisted into something unrecognizable. "Listen, you can hear them already. The accusations. Can you hear them?"

She cocked her head to one side. "What are you talking about? What accusations?"

"You slitty-eyed, urine-complexioned Chink!" I shouted, my voice hoarse. *"You dour-faced, inscrutable monkey, you yellow-faced toothy smile with fortune cookie in hand running with evil intent around town at night. Oh, China-boy, what have you done to our children? What have you done to our children?"*

She retreated into the corner as if each of my words pushed her there. For a few moments, she stared wide-eyed at me, slightly bent over as if she'd just taken a blow to the gut. Then she spoke, finally. "Xing," she said, her voice hitching with grief, "why do you hate yourself so much?"

Just then, her cell phone rang, blaring out a popular love song. It startled both of us. "It's Jason again," she said, turning her back to me. "Hold on." Naomi had always stood with excellent posture, but as the seconds went by, her back straightened and stiffened into a razorblade. She murmured into the phone, one hand cupped over the mouthpiece. She started whispering in frantic hushes.

A wailing siren, faint, cried out in the night outside.

Naomi didn't hear it. The phone in her hand started to tremble. She stole a quick glance at me, then walked into the kitchen, whispering into the phone.

I waited for her in the living room, snow dripping off my clothes, the way I'd waited for her all my life. With utmost patience. Waited, even as the snow kicked up outside, even after I sensed she'd already hung up. Waiting for her to come back to me.

The kitchen was dark when I walked in five minutes later. She was sitting in the corner, cradling the phone, her face contorted and drained. She did not notice me at first, did not see me observing her trembling lips, her closed eyes, her shell-shocked face. Her left arm, almost a separate entity, hung draped across her chest like a consoling snake. Snowflakes on the window dotted shadows on her face, splattered spiders across the bridge of her nose and cheeks.

"What did he say?" I asked.

She jumped at the sound of my voice, out of her chair. Her eyes flicked to me then quickly away. "It's all over the news now." Her voice was sapped of life but jittery with alarm.

"About Jan Blair. Accusing me?"

"Not only that," she said. She paused for a long time, leaning against the window, still unable to look at me. Her next words, though whispered, dropped out of her mouth like heavy burdens. "The police, they found blood on that gravity knife they confiscated from you. The one they found in your backpack. Bloodstains on the handle, on the blade. Blood with a DNA match with at least two of...them, the victims."

"And I told you about the knife. Didn't I just tell you about the knife?"

She shook her head.

"No, I did," I insisted. "I told you..." My voice trailed off with uncertainty. "I did, you weren't..." I paused. She was staring down, keeping her eyes away from me. But watchful.

And so, in my fear, I started to ramble. Gooey bands of saliva stretched between my chapped, ranting lips. My arms flailed, I remember that, gesticulating up and down. Snow in my hair had melted, and water dripped down my face like nervous sweat.

"Jan gave it to me as a gift. I didn't want—"

Naomi put her hand up, stopping me. Her fingers trembled slightly.

"You didn't hear a thing I just said, did you?" I asked.

She half turned away. "I'm just trying to process all this. I don't know—I don't know what to think."

"You need to know. About the knife. It's not mine. Jan gave it to me as a gift."

"But I asked you," she said. "That very night after the police found it, I asked you about the knife, and you said you had no idea how you got it. You never said anything about Jan giving it to you." She spoke with a strained, raspy voice. "In fact, Xing, why didn't you ever tell me about Jan? What were you trying to hide?"

A muscle under my right eye jerked. "Nothing," I said, wary. "There's nothing between us."

"She's been going around the past few weeks, telling the girls. In the locker room after gym class. About how you and her got it on."

"She's lying."

"About how you're smitten with her. Always wanting to kiss her. Even going to her home in the middle of the night to make out with her."

"That girl has been chasing *me* since day one."

"It's not just her saying so. Mindy Burns was saying how she saw the two of you necking in the auditorium." Naomi ran her hands down her face, pulling the sides of her mouth down. "We used to tell each other everything. Even stupid, insignificant stuff. Why didn't you tell me about Jan Blair?"

"I tried to," I blurted, suddenly recalling. "The very day she first...acted weird on me. I went over to your place to talk to you. Later at night. I wanted to unload, just talk."

She frowned. "When was this?"

"Several weeks back. You won't remember it. You were just going to bed. I didn't want to wake you. So I stayed on the tree."

Her arms folded loosely but quickly across her chest. "You were in the tree? Watching me?"

"I...I...it's not like that—"

"From outside my window?"

"Naomi—"

"How long were you out there for?"

I should have lied. I should have just punched out a rough number, two minutes, three minutes. But stupidly I told her the truth. "Two hours."

She stepped back, away from me.

It was a slow, cautious step.

Her left hand slowly rose to her chin, shaking, trembling. She did that whenever she was scared, from the time she was just a little girl. I'd seen her do that dozens of times, but never, not once, on account of me. Her eyes were wide and incredulous. "And you were just watching me for two hours?"

I stammered, I spluttered. But she'd stopped listening.

"Xing," she said. She could hardly get the next words out: "I barely feel like I know you anymore. The way you've been acting." She was blinking fast now. "Let's call the police. Let them know you're here. They just want to talk." I hated that modulated, clipped voice. She was learning to use it now to cut people off in Sunday school or to command the undivided attention of a noisy church youth meeting. She would no doubt later use it to turn down college dates or invitations for a drink on business trips, her voice pert and professional in every inflection. But oh so condescending and patronizing.

"What the hell just happened?" I glared at her. "Ten minutes ago, you wouldn't believe I had anything to do with this. Now you're ready to handcuff me yourself."

"It's not like that."

"No, no. I get it. I totally do. I can scream and rant, and not sway you. The way it's always been." I smirked. "Then one phone call from honey buns, one sweet whisper from your goody white boyfriend, and he has you at hello. Just like that, a total one-eighty." I nodded my head. "I get it."

"Xing, please, just let me call the police, OK?"

"No, that's fine, don't believe me, Naomi," I said. "Others will believe me. Like Miss Durgenhoff."

"Xing," she said, remembering something, her eyes widening.

"She'll speak up for me; she'll tell everyone that I had nothing to do with the murders."

And one last time, Naomi said, "Xing."

I looked at her. Tears were brimming from half-closed eyes. And she began to speak, softly, her wavering voice just barely under control. "I stopped by your home after school today," she said. "I wanted to wish you luck, that even if I couldn't be there..." She sniffed and ran the back of her hand against her nose. "But when I got to your home, everyone was gone except Miss Durgenhoff. She invited me in for some tea."

Sirens in the background, getting louder.

"You know," she continued, "she told me a few things that really surprised me."

I blinked.

"She told me that she's seen you sneak out of the house late at night, only to return hours later. Lots of times. That she's seen you come back caked in dirt and mud, seen you come back disheveled, like you've been in a fight. She tells me that you roam the streets all the time, early in the mornings, in the middle of the night, the only person in the whole town unafraid to do so. I didn't think much of what she said until now...you're acting so weird, you're not yourself. You're scaring me."

I should have said something, some kind of self-defense: That Miss Durgenhoff is old and greatly exaggerates. That although I have been out late at night—and yes, on one occasion I did go to Jan's house in the middle of the night—I did not kill anyone. That I have been leaving home in the morning dark, but only for my voice lessons at school. That I have roamed the streets at night, but only because I hate my own home, only because I'm still trying to find my home.

Naomi's eyes, brown and morose, pierced into me. "What have you been doing?" She whispered it in a slurred hiss, all her syllables spilling in messy overlaps. "Where have you been

going at night? You say you're busy practicing, but what
have you been doing, really?"

My arms dropped to my side. I hadn't realized I'd folded
them taut against my chest. I closed my eyes, pleading for
this world to disappear. A pressure began to pound the back
of my eyeballs.

I wanted to scream. Instead, I opened my eyes.

"Even you, Naomi?"

She stood there, a waif silhouetted against the bleeding
darkness of the night outside, the snow tattering down behind her, unable to answer me. Naomi, like the world, had
made up her mind about me.

I went to her now, for the first time, the last time. I placed
my hand in the small hollow of her back, just above her hips.
It surprised me, the sudden dip then rise of her curve there
in my palm. A hint of how she would mature; a person I
would never be a part of. I lowered my face into the enclave
of her neck and held her. She was stiff and unyielding, and I
waited for her to relent, soften. She never did. Past the fresh
fragrance of her hair, I smelled something more indelible: the
warm waft of her body heat, the raw musk it carried. I never
forgot that smell.

*I wish you could have seen me tonight, Naomi. I wish you could
have seen me at the police precinct. For a couple of hours, I was a
hero. The cameras clicking. The handshakes. The pats on the back.
And I wish you could have been at school to see me perform. I was
magical. I made the angels listen. I was beloved.* These were my
unwhispered words.

I moved past her and opened the door. And just like that,
I walked out.

★

Snow. So much of it coming down, white specks flickering in the dark night like fireworks in disarray, without color,
sapped of passion, drained.

And so I pedaled, even when going downhill, even around
the tight corners. The snow hurtled into my face. Once or
twice, I felt the tires give under me, skidding a foot before
they found traction. I sped over branches and rocks and pot-
holes, my teeth knocking together like a chattering fool, the
slicing cold raw against my face. I heard sirens breaking into
the night air, howling yelps of urgency. This is what you do,
this is how you feel, this is how you maneuver through a
snowy night when all that you have ever prized is irretriev-
ably lost.

THE SECRET PAINTING

The house was dark and cold and empty.

"Ah-ma?" I asked into the darkness, knowing full well that only silence would answer.

I walked through the living room, up the stairs, down the short hallway, letting the silence seep into me, the darkness bleed into me.

I stumbled into my room. This was the room, which had over the years borne a loneliness never meant to be shouldered by only one person. The walls, the bed, the ceiling, the desk, the cluttered books, the discarded clothes—all drenched with the witness of unwept tears.

I heard the wail of sirens, nearer to me than they'd been all night, the screeching of brakes, the shout of voices. Soon they would break into the house, smashing the windows, splintering the front door with a battering ram. Then boots would pound up the stairs. They'd flow into my room like a black river, pull me to the floor, twist my arms back. I would offer no resistance.

They'd tell me I had the right to remain silent. But I would not be silent. I would speak; I would confess to a lie.

Dorsey had screamed.

Barnes had cried.

Hasbourd had pleaded.

Logan had fought back, viciously, like a stray dog.

Jan's father was easy as slicing warm butter.

From downstairs came loud thumps against the door. Only a few moments more now. Let them come. Let them come and get me. I'd give them what they wanted, what they'd already concluded. If even Naomi would not believe me, then how could I ever expect them to?

I walked across the room towards my father's painting.

I took the painting down. Exposed now on the wall was the thin, L-shaped wood panel. My fingers, still frozen, felt clumsily for the edges and loosened the panel. I took out the pouch with my getaway money and poured the contents on my bed. Loose change and cash spilled out, all the folly and futility of a pipe dream. And Logan's gold chain. The gold chain permeated the gray hues of the room, a living color. The initials *TL* on the small plate glowed with radiance, twinkling. As if still alive, alive even after it had been hidden in the dark so many months before. It wrapped itself around my wrist, between my fingers, a sickly embrace. And I closed my hand gently around it, then tighter, into a fist where the chain would no doubt be discovered. It was all they would need, the smoking gun they were slobbering to find.

I placed the painting back up on the wall. And I heard the splintering of wood downstairs as the front door exploded inwards. The shouts of police as they poured in. Mere seconds more now. I stared at the painting in front of me. And it drew me in, as I somehow knew it would. I caressed the encrusted paint, frozen like the waves of an arctic sea. I closed my eyes. Gently now, my fingertips roaming over the canvas. Touching. Slowly. The scent of flowers, the aroma of wet rocks, even the faint sound of willows brushed lightly by the wind. These all came to me, the place of my home. I kept my eyes closed.

The sounds and smells grew stronger, more vivid now; soon I felt the rays of the China sun intensifying upon my face, warm and beckoning. My fingers pressed harder into the canvas. I inhaled and shuddered.

CROSSING TO AMERICA

*I*t is night when they leave China. Xing and his family stand on a rocky beach, waiting. The air is hot and drenched with humidity. A low rumble of thunder sounds from afar even though the dusk sky is clear. They watch as the horizon turns pink with the setting sun, then orange, then purple. Finally, from behind an outlying island comes the ship within which they will spend the next few weeks crossing the seas.

When it becomes clear that the ship isn't going to send out a raft to fetch them, they wade into the water. It is delightfully cool, refreshing against Xing's sweaty skin. His parents abandon on the beach suitcases they spent weeks carefully packing. There are paintbrushes and paintings, his father's most treasured possessions, his very identity, left behind. His father puts Xing on his back. "Hang on, don't let go," his father says.

It is a delicious ride at first, his father's sinewy body propelling them both forward, his mother swimming next to them with one arm raised above the water, holding a bag. But the water turns turbulent, choppy; water splashes into Xing's eyes, its saltiness stinging. And his father weakens; he moves with less propulsion now, his face sometimes sinking underwater for a few frightening seconds. His mother discards the bag she is holding, letting it sink into the murky depths *as she struggles to swim. Her hair is plastered on her face like wet seaweed.*

His father sputters words for Xing to shout at the ship. "Don't leave, we're almost there! We'll give you more money! We're almost there!" And dutifully, Xing shouts these words at the top of his lungs until his voice grows hoarse. When he can no longer shout, when he feels his father's strength fading, he bends down low to his father's ear and whispers. He whispers all those words his father has told him over the years, promises and dreams about America spoken over dumplings, in the fishing raft, on the bicycle, words of hope and success and money and a magical, amazing life.

"We are going to America, Ah-Ba. We are almost there. Just a few more strokes. We can do it. We are almost in America, Ah-Ba."

When they reach the ship, a rope ladder is thrown down. His parents cling to it, relieved but momentarily too exhausted to climb. But Xing grabs one rung after another and hoists himself up onto the deck where he lies sprawled, his body dripping with water. He can feel the ship under him revving its engine for the long crossing ahead. Xing opens his eyes and looks up at the shining stars.

THE END

AUTHOR BIOGRAPHY

Half-Chinese and half-Japanese, Andrew Xia Fukuda was born in New York and raised in Hong Kong. After returning to America, he earned his bachelor's degree in history from Cornell University. Later, he went on to work in Manhattan's Chinatown with immigrant youth, whose struggles for acceptance in predominantly white America inspired him to write *Crossing*, his first novel. In 2009, *Crossing* was a semifinalist in Amazon's Breakthrough Novel Contest. Today he lives on Long Island with his wife and their two sons.